LIVING THINGS

LIVING THINGS

A NOVEL

—

Landon Houle

RED HEN PRESS | *PASADENA, CA*

Book design by Mark E. Cull

Library of Congress Cataloging-in-Publication Data

Names: Houle, Landon, 1985– author.
Title: Living things : stories / Landon Houle.
Description: Pasadena, CA : Red Hen Press, [2019]
Identifiers: LCCN 2019018063 | ISBN 9781597098397
Subjects: LCSH: South Carolina—Fiction.
Classification: LCC PS3608.O85544 A6 2019 | DDC 813/.6—dc23
LC record available at https://lccn.loc.gov/2019018063

The National Endowment for the Arts, the Los Angeles County Arts Commission,
the Ahmanson Foundation, the Dwight Stuart Youth Fund, the Max Factor Family
Foundation, the Pasadena Tournament of Roses Foundation, the Pasadena Arts &
Culture Commission and the City of Pasadena Cultural Affairs Division, the City
of Los Angeles Department of Cultural Affairs, the Audrey & Sydney Irmas Chari-
table Foundation, the Kinder Morgan Foundation, the Meta & George Rosenberg
Foundation, the Allergan Foundation, the Riordan Foundation, Amazon Literary
Partnership, and the Mara W. Breech Foundation partially support Red Hen Press.

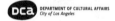

First Edition
Published by Red Hen Press
www.redhen.org

ACKNOWLEDGMENTS

I wish to thank and gratefully acknowledge the following publications on whose pages some of these stories first appeared: "There You Are" appeared in *Dogwood*, Spring 2018; "Living Things" appeared in *Masters Review*, Summer 2016.

CONTENTS

LIVING THINGS

PROLOGUE

It's late, but the girl is still here.

She's still here with Old Man and Sister. Old Man with the twisted foot, Old Man asleep in the chair, and the girl and Sister at the teacher's desk. Sister's hair loose and yellow under the drafting lamp. Sister's hands gone to claws. Say Sister, the girl speaks. But Sister makes not to hear, and the girl rolls her lips, quits.

For her, a chipped cup, and for Sister, a platter of beads from which she plucks. Holds one to the bulb. The threads inside, thick blue ropes and some red.

The girl's hand on her belly. The girl's hand on the cup. Old Man snores and chokes, and Sister says, The way it turns.

She moves the bead, and through it, the girl sees veins, cut glass, some small living flash.

It isn't nothing, Sister says.

How, Old Man says in his sleep.

Sister pulls the thread through her mouth.

Old Man says, How, and the girl starts.

Old Man says, Now, and the girl grinds her teeth.

Now, Now.

Platter and cup. Thin spinning leaf.

What'll happen? the girl says.

And Sister studies what she's making. See there, she answers. See the way they all catch.

A NEW CALIBRATION

Still morning but for the worse. The quarter sun bore down on the dew, and the town sweltered and shone. To some eyes, it was lovely, dull things asparkle—hydrants and dumpsters and the trashy little signs that marked the shops around the square—but what glittered couldn't last in such heat. What now was shining was one morning closer to rusting all the way through.

Already, May Fly felt the damp heat creeping up the seams of her shirt. The festival was in full swing, and something was flapping in May Fly's head so that she was light enough to very nearly float above the oily asphalt. The world before her shimmered and went fuzzy, particularly when she found herself standing in the steam of the barbecue pit, the grill whereon various slabs of still-bloody meat recognizable as hips and legs and wings dripped and spat.

She'd had last night three-quarters of a bottle of cherry cough medicine and perhaps this made the day louder than it would have been otherwise. Preacherman on the corner playing his sermon songs from some strung-up speakers. A small dog barking. And there at the courthouse a lady they called the Spin-Wife telling everybody to stand up, to put their hands together.

May Fly ducked down and moved through the people, some she recognized, others she didn't. It was a little like swimming, which she wished she was doing just now, diving under the blue water at the city pool, moving so fast, so easily against all that weight. She tried to remember the sudden chill, the sharp burn in her nose even as the edges of the iridescent world before her spun in ways they shouldn't have. She hadn't eaten since yesterday's bologna.

Viva said they could go somewhere real nice once May Fly did what she had to do.

Pizza? May Fly said, and Viva said, Yeah. Whatever.

May Fly was in the front yard of the courthouse where they had hauled in some metal bleachers for the kids and the old folks. All the great and great-great grannies were down on the first couple of rows, petrified women with knitted blankets on their laps, fossilized faces nearly hidden under sun hats and black wraparound glasses.

Mama Powell, May Fly's grandmother, was too young for this crowd. She'd be over at the church, selling her pies and changing money for the benefit sale. May Fly wouldn't have to worry about Mama Powell. Viva had promised that.

This was the talent show, and on stage a boy in a store-bought sheriff's costume played a plastic recorder. It was more squeaks than notes, but just to the side of the stage, Spin-Wife bobbed and tapped as if the racket was a familiar tune. When it was over, when the boy took the recorder away from his mouth in a great string of spittle, Spin-Wife told everybody to give it up for Little Charlie Whitehead.

May Fly clapped, but she kept moving. She wasn't here to watch the talent show or listen to Preacherman or play the carnival games, though she did, for a minute, linger in front of the balloon booth—all those animals on strings, a giant stuffed dog which she liked in particular and fancied even more for the way one eye was so clearly sewn upside down. She studied that dog for some time, but then a man threw a dart and a balloon popped and May Fly flinched as if she'd been asleep standing up. She slapped her face, a bug she felt crawling there. She was back now, back to where she had no choice but to be.

May Fly didn't have money to pop balloons, but Viva said what she was doing was a kind of game. There was a set of plastic checkers at the house, and since Viva didn't want to play—Ain't good at that sort of stuff, she said—May Fly learned to play herself. That is, she played a different version of herself. One May Fly was careful and thought a long time about her next play. But the other May Fly took more risks. Sometimes she moved without thinking. Sometimes she just jumped.

Viva said, You look at that board. You're making sure you see everything, she said. Right?

Viva flicked May Fly on the ear. Hear me, girl? she said, and May Fly nodded.

That's right, Viva said. It's the same thing. You're gonna look around, check things out. You're gonna figure out when and where to move. And then, Viva clapped in May Fly's face, you get the prize.

May Fly listened and when Viva asked if she understood, May Fly said, How come you can't go? Why's it gotta be me?

Viva laughed and her silver tooth caught the light in a way that made it look black. Her hair, when she had it done, fell in tight little curls but was, just now, a series of tangles and rats. Viva shook it off her face but it fell right back. Because, she said, people notice me.

Loose lines of snickering teenagers and mothers with strollers and bored finger-snapping men trudged around May Fly. They scratched at bugs and made faces at babies and ate meat off sticks, plodding from table to table as if in chutes, as if they too had no other place to go. The vendors were set up in stalls around the square, and there was Preacherman, and there were games, and there was a gray-headed woman from the waste water department passing out pamphlets about rain barrels. There were handicrafts—tables lined with ugly wooden toys and signs decorated with cute sayings: HOME IS WHERE THE MESS IS. And there in front of the Merle Norman was Miss Rawley, the plant woman.

May Fly knew Miss Rawley, had been to see her one Saturday afternoon with Mama Powell. Miss Rawley lived with her mother and sold plants out of a clapboard which, at one point, had been painted a patriotic blue but was now more weathered wood than anything. To her credit, Miss Rawley probably didn't know the difference. The house might have been in pristine condition as far as she knew because Miss Rawley had a beautiful pair of smoky eyes that were like most pretty things in that they were nearly useless. One eye, jewel that it was, even had a tendency to wander back toward the bone, and when Mama Powell asked how much is this one, Miss Rawley had to feel the leaves. She had to feel the little knotted buds to know that it was a geranium.

Miss Rawley's mother was still mobile, but she was white-haired and tiny and couldn't have been any younger than eighty-five, and she spent most of her time in a lawn chair underneath a shade tree where every branch was hung with a homemade wind chime.

She's blind, May Fly said when they were back in the car. The backseat was full of red geraniums, and though they didn't smell exactly, there was what you could call an odor of dirt and greenery and living things. She's blind and she plants all those plants.

Mama Powell looked like she was shaking her head, but she was also looking both ways not once but twice before she pulled out onto Main. Some things, she said, you don't need to see to know.

At the festival, May Fly didn't bother hiding even though Viva said she needed to make sure nobody saw. May Fly just stood in the middle of things, her hard flat belly sweating through the screened faces of three Disney princesses. Her eyes shifted and worked. There was old Miss Rawley selling chimes from her lawn chair, and the younger Miss Rawley feeling her way through the pots. She stooped to touch this leaf or that dirt. Some of the pots she watered from a rusting can. There was a lawn chair for her too, and underneath was the purse that held the billfold from which, May Fly saw, Miss Rawley was making change.

This place is stupid, Viva had said, and May Fly knew she didn't mean Black Creek exactly. A place couldn't be stupid or smart or rich or poor or black or white or good or bad. A place was only what it was, and May Fly understood that Viva meant the people. They don't watch out for things. They don't think anything bad's gonna happen ever.

They were in the living room. Viva was on the couch, and May Fly was on the floor with her cheek pressed up against Viva's leg.

They think, Viva said, everything's just gonna be happily ever after. She made a hissing sound. Air funneled around that silver tooth. Maybe for them that's true.

Viva had a paper party plate balanced on her knee. She was breaking up a bud, and for May Fly, who'd seen this maybe a hundred times, her mother's hands might have been snapping peas for supper. She moved her head so that her ear was tight against her mother's skin. In science class, they'd talked some about bodies, nothing anybody really wanted to know but just some vague stuff about bones and veins and blood. May Fly pretended she could hear these things moving and working. She could hear everything that was inside of her mother.

I used to be that way, Viva said. I used to think everything would be okay. You learn, though. And I learned that good and quick.

What May Fly could feel without pretending was the vibration of her mother's voice. She could feel that in the knee and the bone. She rubbed her fingers against her mother's skin. She smelled the weed, the earth in it. It was better than the other stuff Viva sometimes smoked, the junk that reeked like burnt marshmallows and a pan somebody left on the stove.

People like us, Viva said, we got to make our own good.

May Fly blinked and squinted against the brighter light. On stage, Spin-Wife was asking how everybody was doing this morning. She was yelling at them. Come on! she screamed at the grannies. You can do better than that!

A higher sun, and May Fly's mind startled into a wild starving flutter. For a minute, she wasn't sure what she was doing. For a minute, she only saw the auras of things—a glowing Miss Rawley mottled by dark blotches, the shadows of leaves and black spots for black pieces.

And red for red, Mama Powell said. She'd been the one to teach May Fly how to play which sometimes, she said, amounted to biding your time. It might seem like you've got yourself stuck in a corner, but you don't. You're just waiting, see there. You just need the right opportunity.

May Fly opened her eyes wide, and she swallowed until the spots disappeared, and it wasn't long—ten minutes, a half hour—before old Miss Rawley pushed herself up and out of the lawn chair. She stood without moving, and around her, the metal chimes flashed in the sun, and for a few terrible seconds, old Miss Rawley, framed in all that glare, was staring right at May Fly. But she was only regaining her balance, letting the blood back into her legs as Mama Powell did when she'd been sitting too long.

Old Miss Rawley pulled up the waist of her pants and took a few tentative steps toward the younger Miss Rawley. They reached out to each other, and stood there, the one holding up the other. Then old Miss Rawley let go and set off in a slow and painful hobble in the direction of the porta-potties.

On stage, the next act was a troupe of dancers May Fly's own age, and if she'd looked, she'd have recognized a few of them as homeroom classmates. They gathered in formation, their little fingers on the brims of their costume top hats. The music began, and it was a loud poppy number, a voice more robot than human. The feet stomped in a kind of brigade, and up close, the song played loud enough to chatter the speakers, but May Fly didn't see her classmates. And as she moved in, what she heard, even louder than the music, was all those wind chimes. Most of them were made of forks and knives hammered flat, and in some winds, they made a sound that was less musical than frantic, and Mama Powell, who'd spent a number of years in Oklahoma, told May Fly once that when she heard that clattering, she couldn't think of anything but tornadoes. The way the wind blew and the sky turned yellow, and you knew you better hunker down. You knew a bad one was coming.

On stage, the children were dancing, and at Miss Rawley's booth, a couple with a baby was looking at a nice rose bush. Miss Rawley went over to them, and May Fly knew she was telling them what a rose liked and didn't like. Miss Rawley was talking about the rose like it was a person, like it was capable of feeling and thought and action all its own. May Fly knew what Miss Rawley was saying even before she could hear it with her own ears, even before she was ducking down and swiping the red leather billfold and tucking it into the loose waist of her shorts.

Lady Banks, Miss Rawley said, will outlive your grandchildren.

May Fly was sliding around Miss Rawley now.

She smells just like violets.

Miss Rawley knew the geranium well enough, not just by touching it but by sniffing the air, a scent May Fly had tried to catch. So maybe Miss Rawley *did* know that her house needed painting, and maybe she knew that May Fly was close. Maybe there was something about May Fly that could be sensed without seeing.

Suddenly, the music came to a quick stop, and there was the thud of so many bodies, seven sets of show-stopping splits. In the thin applause that ensued, May Fly nearly ran but held herself to a fast walking clip.

The Spin-Wife said, Make some noise for The Stars and Stripes!

May Fly thought she heard somebody yelling. She thought she heard somebody calling after her, but she told herself it was just Preacherman. Preacherman was calling after everybody all the time, saying the world was gonna end, and they were all going to hell unless they stood up, unless they took that first step, Lord. And he was singing now, Preacherman was. They had to ask. They had to get on their knees and beg for forgiveness! Please, Lord, Preacherman sang. Give me life!

Things were turning in May Fly's stomach, but she kept walking. She did what Viva told her. She didn't turn around.

≈

On TV, when they had TV, May Fly had seen the way suicide bombing worked. She'd only caught the last half-hour of the movie, and she didn't understand why the man did what he did, only how he did it. The way he put on a vest strapped with dynamite. How he moved like old Miss Rawley, like a person in pain as he made his way into a tall building constructed, it seemed, entirely of mirrors. The man in the movie said a prayer in another language and nodded as if in some response just before he reached inside his coat and pressed the button.

May Fly felt Miss Rawley's red billfold, hot and sticky against her belly. She stuck her hands in her pockets, holding up her baggy shorts as she walked—struggling not to run—the five blocks from the square, past the paper mill, and down the tracks to the little white house with the dirt yard where she and Viva stayed. Viva said it wouldn't be any different than checkers, but May Fly felt more like the man in the movie. Like, at any minute, everything might explode.

Viva was on the porch, and, May Fly saw that Fat Greg was there with her. Fat Greg was short and fat and wore shirts and shorts of the same color so that, with his bald head and his thick wrists, he looked like an ugly old baby in pajamas.

One time May Fly said as much to her mother, and Viva snorted, but then her face was serious, and she said for May Fly not to say anything like that to Fat Greg ever.

Greg sometimes brought over buckets of chicken, and he licked his fingers when he ate and even when he wasn't eating, and one time, when Viva was doing something in the bathroom, Greg made May Fly hold his gun even though she didn't want to. He made her point it at a brown bird that was building a nest up under the porch, and then he said, Pow! And when May Fly jumped, when she dropped the gun, he slapped the back of her head. She was just like her mama. She'd fool around and hurt herself if she wasn't careful.

Just now, Greg was taking up the better part of the rusted glider which was one of May Fly's favorite places. He was smoking, and so was Viva, but when she saw May Fly coming up the road, Viva threw down the cigarette and smashed it under her sandal.

Took you long enough, Viva said. She came down the cement steps so quick she hung her shoe in a crack. She tripped, and when May Fly felt her mother's hands on her shoulders, there was weight behind them as if some part of Viva were still falling, still trying to get her balance.

But Viva kept her feet. It was May Fly who almost went down when Viva yanked hard on her T-shirt. Viva was pulling the shirt nearly up over May Fly's head, and May Fly felt the sticky billfold peeling off her belly and the hot sun on her bare skin. Even though May Fly was just eight, Viva kept saying they needed to get her a bra, but they hadn't yet, and now May Fly was sure Greg had just seen her bare chest. She yelled and jerked away, pulling down her shirt so hard the neck got stretched, and ever after, the faces of those princesses were as lined and loose as the courthouse grannies'.

On the porch, Greg was laughing, a kind of gristled choke that changed to a cough. She thinks, he sputtered. She thinks she's got something to see.

May Fly held her shirt down. She pressed her lips into a hard knot.

Viva had Miss Rawley's wallet. Let's see what you got, Viva said. What's the prize, I mean. She winked at May Fly, and a muscle flinched in her neck. Viva was wearing the necklace she always wore, but something about the beads reminded May Fly of the stuffed dog, the eye that was all wrong.

Hot out here, Viva said, and when she headed back up to the porch, May Fly kicked at the dirt like she might do something. But then she just followed her mama and sat down hard on the cement steps with her chin on her hand. Her head was hurting as it sometimes did mornings after she drank the cherry syrup. She'd done what she had to do, and she was home now, and nothing had exploded, but a part of May Fly suddenly wished that it would.

You gonna say hi to your Uncle Greg? Greg said. He sucked on the cigarette.

Nope, May Fly said.

May Fly, Viva said.

He ain't my uncle.

Greg blew smoke and squinted at May Fly. Then what am I?

Viva shot May Fly a look that said shut your mouth. From the wallet, she'd pulled out several white envelopes. They weren't sealed, and May Fly watched as Viva took out what was inside. Several ones and fives. A ten and a twenty.

One fifty even. Viva stuffed the envelopes back in the wallet and held up the cash.

She grinned at May Fly. Then she bent down and kissed her. You did it, girl. You made the good.

Can I have that? May Fly said, and she pointed at the wallet.

Viva looked at it, turned it over as if she was deciding. Then she handed it to May Fly. All yours. Go play shopper, she said. Play like you're a lady.

May Fly took the wallet. She'd held it before, but now she really felt it, the smooth leather that was almost like touching something alive.

Ha! Viva said. She was counting the money. There's more than a hundred here.

Ha! Greg said, and he was mocking Viva, making fun of her now. Which means you only need a hundred more.

It was a little porch, and when Greg reached out and took the money, he didn't even have to get up. He stayed right where he was, sprawled across the glider, and just reached out and took the cash from Viva. Easy as that.

May Fly gripped the wallet. She looked back at her mother, waiting for her to do something, but Viva just stood there with her jaw hanging loose and her hand still up in the air, holding a bunch of nothing.

Mama! May Fly said like she was trying to wake Viva up, and Viva closed her mouth, but she didn't say anything. May Fly stood up and took the last step so now she was on the porch too, and she said to Greg, Give that back. That's ours.

Greg made a face, a kind of terrible grin. Or what?

Or, May Fly said, and she gritted her teeth, and Greg snorted, but this time, he didn't choke. This time, he said to Viva, Look at your pup. She's ready to fight!

He growled at May Fly. He showed his teeth. Then he barked at her.

May Fly pulled back, but the noise snapped something in Viva. That's bullshit, she said. You're bullshit, Greg, and you know it.

Greg's eyes rolled around. What I know is what you owe. And what you owe is a lot more than this.

I paid already, Viva said.

You paid a payment, Greg said.

Viva nodded. Yeah. That's what I'm telling you.

Don't you know? Greg said. Every loan carries an interest.

Beside the glider was a metal plant stand. May Fly's grandmother had one just like it where now sat one of Miss Rawley's red geraniums. But Viva didn't care nothing about plants. Viva, Mama Powell had said more than once, doesn't care nothing about nothing.

There was just an empty stand and metal as it was, nothing really happened. Nothing broke when Viva reached out and turned it over. She worked her mouth like she couldn't think of what to say. Or maybe there wasn't anything to say.

The stand rolled around there on the porch, and they all watched it with a kind of patience, a dull curiosity that occupies those used to watching wheels and anything else that spins. When it finally stopped, when it finally got wedged up against the rail of the porch, Greg said, I know how you can settle up. Maybe even have some left over.

May Fly was close enough to hear them both breathing. She looked at Viva. The plant stand was all curlicues and whatnots, and it weighed hardly anything. Still, pushing it over had taken something out of Viva. All the sudden, she looked spent. She looked like she might fall down if somebody didn't find her a chair.

Mama, May Fly said.

Greg stuck his thumb in his mouth and pulled it out again. You say the word.

Viva's eyes closed, and just when May Fly thought they might stay that way, they opened again. Not now, she said.

Greg stuck out his tongue.

Viva took in air. Then not here, she said.

Greg grinned. His eyes nearly disappeared. He threw down the smoke. Between his fingers was the wad of Miss Rawley's money. All right then, he said, and he pushed himself to standing. Behind him, the glider moved back and forth like a part of a clock. Deal.

He took one step, then two. He stopped in front of May Fly, and even though she tried to get away, he reached out and caught her chin. He said, I had me a pup one time.

Viva had her back turned. She was staring at a crack in the cement.

She was always wanting to run off somewhere, Greg said. Thought she could make it on her own. So I had to chain her up.

Greg's thumb drew a circle around May Fly's lips. She still kept trying to run off. Thought she'd break the chain if she pulled hard enough.

Greg, Viva said.

But all she broke, Greg said, was her own stupid neck.

Greg's thumb was on May Fly's chin. He tapped once, twice. Then he jerked her head in the other direction, twisting her neck hard.

Stop it, Viva said. She'd spun around and now her fists were balled up and she was hitting Greg in the back—stop it, stop it, stop it—but it was like punching a mattress, something May Fly could do until she wore herself out, and nothing changed except the next day her arms might be sore. You don't touch her ever, Viva said, and she hit Greg until she was out of breath, until he turned around and looked at her.

He could hit her, May Fly thought. He could kill her even.

Greg stared hard and said, Be in the truck. Slowly, whistling, he made his way down the stairs and around the house.

Viva and May Fly stood there, wide-legged and balled-fisted, panting on the porch, and anyone who saw them would have thought they were the ones fighting, and of course, in some ways, they were and always would be. But when Viva's eyes lit back on May Fly, she did her best to smile. I'm gonna get us that pizza, she said.

May Fly turned her head. She looked out toward the tracks. Every day the trains came. She didn't know where they came from or where they went when they were gone. May Fly watched them from the glider, and sometimes Viva sat with her. Viva said she'd been hearing those trains all her life. She'd been hearing them so long she didn't even listen anymore.

Look at me, Viva said and said until May Fly finally turned her head and looked, and she didn't want Viva to see her face, but there was no way around it. Her nose burned, and she thought again of being in the water, how under the surface, all the sounds were muffled. If she were swimming, she wouldn't be able to hear her mother. She wouldn't be able to understand the words, When I get back. While I'm gone. Promise.

There was hardly any softness left to Viva. She was all bones and angles so that later, when May Fly missed her mother more than she ever thought you could miss a person, she'd press her face against the edge of a table or her school desk until she cut a line in her cheek.

Sausage or pepperoni, Viva said. Be thinking.

And then she was gone, sandals slapping against the dirt yard, the pop and slam of the truck door. A plum flash in the sun and from the stereo, a thudding bass May Fly felt as a rattle in her chest. Like Little Charlie Whitehead and every other second grader, May Fly had learned to play the recorder. It was the music teacher that told the class how if you listened to music loud enough, it could hurt your ears. It could actually change the rhythm of your heart. She felt that shifting now, a new calibration that left her short of breath and more than a little dizzy.

A breeze came up from the south, and in the trees, the leaves shook and turned. May Fly sat down on the glider. She opened the wallet, took out the empty envelopes. She studied them—sniffed the glue. She ran her fingers along the edges until she felt the notches. It took her a minute to figure it out. She closed her eyes. One cut for ones. Two cuts for fives. Three cuts for tens. Four cuts for the twenties.

This and everything about the wallet made a certain kind of sense. Miss Rawley had a photo identification card. May Fly slipped it out of the plastic sleeve. In the picture, Miss Rawley was wearing pink lipstick, and her teeth were very white, and somehow when the camera flashed, she'd known right where to look.

It was more than just a breeze. The wind was picking up, and from the square, May Fly could hear someone speaking into a microphone. Clouds were rolling in, and the sun came through in rays, and if you were closer to the center of town, the words would be loud and clear, but this far away, the voice seemed to come from up above, like distant thunder, and you couldn't understand a thing no matter how hard you tried.

≈

May Fly had trouble sleeping, which was why she sometimes drank the cherry syrup. Then sometimes she drank the syrup just because it was what there was to do. That afternoon, though, she must have been too worn out all of a sudden to keep herself awake wondering about things like blood in the body and where her daddy was and what would happen if her mama didn't come home. She must have been too spent to keep her eyes open a minute longer. Otherwise, she would have done more when Mama Powell drove up. She would have thought to hide Miss Rawley's wallet. She would have made up some better lie about where her mother had gone and when she'd be back.

As it was, Mama Powell was screaming before May Fly could get her eyes open good. Mama Powell was a small woman who most often wore loose flowered shifts, but she was still dressed for the yard sale, much like old Miss Rawley in her T-shirt and stretch jeans and fanny pack. Mama Powell's curled wig had slipped down on her head so that her face appeared smaller than it was, and overall, she had the appearance of some furious and rabid rodent shaking Miss Rawley's ID card in May Fly's face.

What are you doing with Miss Rawley's things?

This was the question that, like a second hand passing the twelve, Mama Powell kept circling back to between more questions about Viva and where Viva went and who Viva went with and when Viva would be coming home.

Don't know, May Fly said until she finally covered her ears and just screamed it with enough force to stop even Mama Powell. Mama Powell looked down at May Fly, and May Fly looked up at her, and it was true that Mama Powell was too young to sit with the great-grannies, but that afternoon, she did look aged in ways that May Fly hadn't noticed before. Mama Powell's wig slipped sideways, and her eyes were dark hollows, and when she was finally quiet, her lips sagged as if whatever she was stopping herself from saying bore an extraordinary weight.

She left with Fat Greg, May Fly said. I don't know where.

Mama Powell put her hands on her hips and looked down the street, up and down again, always twice, better safe, she said, than sorry. It was an easy kind of movement, a habit, as if she'd spent a long time looking for Viva to come around a corner. I remember when Greg Ross sold candy for the band, she said.

May Fly watched her grandmother. It seemed like just another thing Mama Powell said that didn't much matter.

Mama Powell let her arms go loose and she sat down beside May Fly in the glider.

You ate something? she said.

May Fly scratched her face. In a corner of the porch was a smear of mud where the nest used to be.

Mama Powell breathed. In her lungs, there was a kind of hum. She was full of odd words and sounds. She smelled like moth balls and the butter lotion she used. I got an extra pie at the house, she said. She patted May Fly on the knee. Mama Powell couldn't sit anywhere very long. Come on, she said. She looked at the wallet but was careful not to touch it. And bring all that mess with you.

Mama Powell's car was still cool from the air conditioning. The carpets had been vacuumed two or three times since they brought the geraniums from Miss Rawley's. There wasn't a trace of dirt anywhere.

It was late in the afternoon, and there hadn't been rain yet but the wind was still up. The clouds were still building. Mama Powell drove back down around the square where most of the vendors, including Miss Rawley, had already pulled up and gone home. Preacherman's speakers were gone, but he was still talking to a few people. He raised his hand, waved as they passed.

I heard him talking, May Fly said, about how the world's gonna end. How it's already ending.

Mama Powell blinked. She rolled her lips.

You think it'll just go dark like nighttime? May Fly said. Or will it explode all of a sudden?

Mama Powell's head sort of trembled, and she reached up, adjusted her wig. You shouldn't be listening to all that, she said. You ought to come to church with me.

He said everybody knows the truth. He's just brave enough to say it out loud, May Fly said.

Loud is right. Loud and proud and flashy. Bad as your mama. That's what he is. Wearing that hat and playing that music. Wants everybody looking at him when we should be looking at the Lord.

Mama Powell glanced at May Fly, and May Fly was staring back.

Mama Powell shifted in her seat and got a better hold on the wheel. What I'm saying is, she said, we got to pay attention to young folks. Young folks ought to be the hope of the nation.

The United States.

Mama Powell hummed. That's right.

That's in the Bible?

Mama Powell held her head high so that her chin pointed at the dash. Something like.

They were off the square now and into a neighborhood. May Fly held Miss Rawley's wallet. She pressed it tight against her stomach. She was hungry. She knew she was, but she didn't feel it anymore. She didn't feel much of anything.

Makeisha, Mama Powell said, you've got to give this up right now. You can't be taking what isn't yours.

May Fly reached for the dash. She wanted to turn on the radio. Sometimes Mama Powell let her turn on the AM. May Fly didn't care what kind of music it was as long as it was loud, but Mama Powell slapped her hand. Girl, she said, you better learn to listen.

They were pulling up to Miss Rawley's now, the falling down house that looked even worse than it did just a few months ago.

Mama Powell sidled up to the curb and cut the engine. Things inside the car popped and hissed and sounded like the workings of Mama Powell herself.

You're gonna give back what you took, she said. You're gonna say you're sorry.

May Fly didn't move until Mama Powell slapped her leg. March! she said.

So May Fly opened the car door and got out and shut it. She held the wallet. She stood there long enough for Mama Powell to flap her hand around and say something May Fly couldn't hear through the glass. Then she turned around and made her way up the busted brick walk and onto the porch.

All around, the chimes rang like so many odd bells. Somewhere, there was thunder.

After a minute, Miss Rawley opened the door. She stayed behind the screen, and May Fly said what she was told to say. She said *something* anyway, but she was thinking about tornadoes, about a story she'd heard Mama Powell telling some of her church friends. Mama Powell got quiet as soon as she saw May Fly was listening, but May Fly had already heard how the tornado had come right down the interstate. A family had taken shelter up underneath an overpass because that's what they tell you to do if you're in a car and such a disaster strikes. You don't have a choice. You get out and you get in the ditch, and that's what this family did, and when it was over, the mother opened her eyes, and all that was in her arms was a blanket. The baby she'd been holding was gone.

Gone? one of Mama Powell's church friends had said. Just like that?

And Mama Powell said that it was. That it was just like that. The baby was gone, and they looked everywhere, and finally they found the poor thing, some fifteen miles away, up in a tree.

Was it alive? the lady said, and Mama Powell said they thought it was. It looked all right, not scratched up or anything, but when they got it down, they saw that the baby was dead.

The church ladies covered their mouths and shook their heads, but they leaned in closer. Was it a head wound? one said. A contusion?

A hematoma?

Mama Powell nodded. Might have been, she said, and she was nearly whispering now. But that wind. It gets so strong. It'll rip off the roof of a house and suck everything out the top.

That's when Mama Powell had seen May Fly watching and she'd gone real quiet real quick, but May Fly had heard the worst of it. Sometimes when she closed her eyes, she thought about her mother and she thought about her daddy, and she thought, too, about birds and wind chimes and babies in trees. And standing there in front of Miss Rawley, she thought she knew what it might feel like to have everything inside of you ripped right out.

Maybe Miss Rawley knew something about that too. She listened to what May Fly had to say. Then she opened the screen and took the wallet back, and she didn't say much of anything besides thank you, but she looked at May Fly. She stared right at her, and it wasn't just the color of Miss Rawley's eyes that made a person feel like she was seeing through to the bottom of something deep and dark.

You hear that? Miss Rawley said.

They stood there together, and neither one of them moved, and they were quiet as people are when they are listening, and there were the chimes, but there was also, from some distance, the rumble and then the unmistakable blow of the train.

Miss Rawley smiled. It's on its way.

She stepped back inside and closed the screen door, and by the time May Fly turned around and walked back down the steps, the train was already that much louder, so much closer. She got into Mama Powell's car, and Mama Powell started the engine, and they drove away. They drove not back to the white house by the tracks but over to Mama Powell's on Quinby Place.

They didn't have pizza. Mama Powell never ate food made in a restaurant, and she wouldn't dream of making something so foreign herself. But she cooked macaroni and cheese and there were collards and there was bread and for dessert, pecan pie.

Mama Powell made May Fly take a bath and gave her an old nightgown to sleep in and rubbed her elbows and her knees with the same butter that she herself used. May Fly stayed in Viva's old room. There wasn't much of Viva left in it, just a few pictures and some dresses in the back of the closet. But there was a certain and strong sense that Viva had been there, had so often slept in the very bed where May Fly lay now. Viva was so much like a ghost in that room that May Fly had to remind herself her mother wasn't dead. Her mother wasn't dead.

It was dark outside, and finally, the rain had started to fall. It came gently at first, and then grew into a steady drum. May Fly had eaten everything Mama Powell had put in front of her, but there was still a distinct sinking, an empty place that would growl for good. May Fly wondered if Miss Rawley had gone through her wallet yet, if she'd noticed what was missing.

Like Mama Powell said, you didn't always need to see to understand. So maybe Miss Rawley knew what May Fly was just figuring out as she laid in bed feeling the sharp cut of the identification card against her hand. You had to give up a lot. Most everything, May Fly saw now. But there were some things you couldn't let go.

SOME THREAT OF EXPLOSION

Miriam was awake and watching, so she saw the hatchback Datsun rattle up and scarcely slow as the rolled newspaper shot out the open window and landed square in the street.

Miriam didn't remember papers thrown in the street when Bobby was alive. In fact, she remembered the newspaper landing precisely in the middle of the welcome mat she kept by the front door. From behind the porch plants, she watched the Datsun speed up as it careened around the corner. A puff of smoke came out the blackened tail pipe, and the smell of it burned Miriam's nose. She had the feeling that people were taking advantage of her. She was a woman, old and alone.

Scoot, she said to the orange cat on her lap. Dutifully, Pete jumped off her lap and stretched his way to the edge of the porch where he began licking his paw in earnest.

Miriam pushed up off the wicker loveseat. It was an old loveseat that she sprayed every spring. This past March, the project had taken the better part of a day because for some reason, a change in medication perhaps, Miriam had felt more worn out than usual. She'd had to sit down halfway through the job and drink some orange juice. On top of the new heart pills, it was just the paint getting to her, all those toxins. Things were more poisonous than they used to be. Miriam was sure of it.

It was 7:38 a.m. Miriam wore her watch though she was still in her nightgown, a cotton smock that, in the sun, showed the rolls and folds of her body, but at that time of day, the neighborhood was quiet. There weren't many people out and about.

Ridiculous, Miriam said. The paper was closer to the neighbor's house than it was to her own. A pair of lesbians lived in the yellow house, and Miriam was surprised at how little this bothered her. She found herself only dimly curious about how Cathy and the other woman came to have a tiny baby. Probably the same way Clarice Powell, another old widow who lived on the other side of Miriam, came to have her little granddaughter living with her. Everything boiled down to someone not taking responsibility while everyone else footed the bill.

Miriam reached down for the paper, and for a minute, there wasn't one paper but two. Miriam closed her eyes tight and shook her head. She made a note to give the circulation manager a call, let him know about the poor state of deliveries, and while she was at it, she might say something about those editorials, which were sometimes engaging but more often than not wound up in a kind of spiritual fervor with all of the principle and none of the grace. Tiresome, Miriam would tell him, and she'd make sure he knew she was a retired language arts teacher and that what she thought mattered. The editorials were a perfect example—they just didn't teach appropriate tone and specific audience in schools anymore, Miriam believed without really knowing what anyone did now. She was seventy-three, and it had been a long time since she'd been in a classroom or anywhere besides church.

She pulled off the rubber band and slid it down her knobby wrist. Still standing in the street, she unrolled the paper as if it were some holy scroll. She studied the big picture on the front page—three young girls wearing crowns and holding bouquets of red roses.

Below the fold, *The Record* had a *What's Happening?* section that listed play productions and concerts and things, mostly in the next town over, and Miriam had intended to go to a few of these events, but she hadn't. Somehow, it had become difficult for her to go places. She was tired at times. That was true, but there was something else. Something more.

Miriam knew a poor shift in tone, and she could still recognize the moment when passion overtook a writer's reason, but there were times when she could hardly imagine that for forty-six years, she'd gone to work every morning and stood in front of so many children looking to her for answers. When Miriam thought of those days, even briefly, she was nearly overcome with a terror so strong it could buckle her knees. So she didn't go to the plays or the concerts or the benefit sales. Instead, she stayed home and pulled a few weeds or, more likely, watched television—cooking shows and British comedies and, when she was feeling really low, afternoon game shows.

Birds of a Feather was on just now, and Miriam was about to turn and go back to the house when, in Cathy's yard, something moved and caught Miriam's eye. For a ridiculous second, Miriam thought she must have seen the baby, but the baby wouldn't be out there alone, would she?

Miriam's perception adjusted and she saw it was Cathy's dog, Spikey. What a dull name, Miriam thought. All together expected and an assault to the dog's worth as far as Miriam was concerned. On principle, Miriam believed that animals should be given the dignity of a normal, respectable name. Nothing food-related like Biscuit or Nacho or Oreo.

Nothing too cute like Cuddles or Snug-Bug. *Spikey* was a cliché and not at all suitable for the mastiff who, despite his monstrous size, seemed very sweet and more rolls and loose skin than muscle. A name like Spikey, Miriam thought to tell Cathy, gave people the wrong impression.

Miriam had only seen Spikey a couple of times when Cathy took him for a walk. He was always in the backyard behind a tall privacy fence Cathy had built. Miriam had been spraying the loveseat—actually, she'd been sitting on the porch, drinking her orange juice—when Cathy was putting up the panels. She and the other woman hadn't had the baby long then, and Miriam thought the fence was a smart move. If you weren't careful, something could happen. You had to take certain measures. You had to protect what you loved.

Spikey's tongue lolled and dripped. He was a huge dog, a hundred pounds or more, but he was gentle.

Miriam called out to him. You thirsty?

Spikey turned, and when he saw Miriam, he seemed to recognize, to remember her. He broke out into an excited run, bounding into the street. But then something else caught in his joints. His wrinkled face changed, and his ears sharpened to points. The short hair along his back stiffened to a ridge of hackles, and instead of running, he leapt, and it wasn't Miriam he was after. It was Pete. Miriam caught a glimpse of Pete in Spikey's mouth, and within her field of vision, things moved in ways they shouldn't have. The pavement flowed like water, like a current that carried Miriam back not only in space but also in time. She was in her house again, and this day slipped back to another horrible day when Miriam was stirring soup how many years ago, and the phone rang, and it was a stranger, and the TV was on, and there was so much noise, Miriam couldn't even tell that then, like now, she was the one screaming.

≈

Somehow Pete got loose from Spikey. Miriam didn't see this. It all happened so fast, and she didn't know it, but as soon as Miriam caught sight of Pete in Spikey's mouth, she'd closed her eyes tight, and in her mind, everything was too loud. There was too much salt in the soup, and she was on the phone, and some woman was saying they'd found a body, that it might be Evie.

So Miriam didn't see Pete break away and run up the electric pole. And he was crouched at the top, twenty-five feet up in the air, his mouth open like a gargoyle's. At the base of the pole, Spikey circled and whined.

Miriam was still in the street, and after some time, she came back to herself, back to the spot where she was rooted, the paper clenched in her hand. A pickup was coming. People drove too fast down Quinby Place. Miriam had phoned the police several times to tell them so. She'd leash-trained Pete so he'd know to use the sidewalk instead of running across the street. But now Miriam was the one in the middle of the road, and she should have moved. She should have gotten out of the way, but instead, she stayed where she was, and as the truck got closer, she held up the hand that still held the newspaper as if she had the power to stop anything.

The man's window was down, and as the truck rolled toward her, he leaned out and spit at the pole and said, That your dog?

Already, Spikey was tired of running himself around in circles. Pete was so high up in the air that from certain angles, you could barely see him. Spikey trotted out into the street. When he heard the man's voice, he jumped up and put his big front paws on the door, looking to be pet.

After a kitty cat, ain't you? the man said. He reached out a rough hand and patted Spikey hard on the head.

Miriam let out a yelp. Her voice shook, but her face was dry. I think he's hurt, she said.

The man wore a John Deere hat and blue suspenders. He growled. He'll be all right. Animals are tough.

He gave Spikey one last bop on the head. It's in their nature, he said, and then the tires were rolling again, perilously close to both the dog and Miriam.

Miriam watched him drive on. The back of the truck was full of junk, a scarred end table, a stationary bike that looked oddly human, like a girl in pig tails. So much looked like what it wasn't.

Miriam tried to see Pete at the top of the pole, but the sun was higher, brighter now. The cicadas were tuning. More time passed than should have before Miriam did what she should have done to begin with, and if it weren't for Pete letting out a low and miserable yowl, she might not have moved at all. But when Miriam heard that call, the very sound of fear and pain, her feet moved and moved quick.

She ran over to Cathy's house, and Spikey followed, close on her heels, and even though he was the one who started this whole mess, he and Miriam now seemed to be working as a team, each doing their part in getting Cathy to the door. Miriam knocked hard and hollered, and behind her, Spikey whined and let out a few desperate barks.

Despite the racket, the door stayed closed, and there was a certain stillness, the sense of no one home.

Miriam whimpered. It wasn't like her to whimper, but sometimes Miriam wasn't herself anymore. Her hands were sweating, and she was wiping them down the front of her thin nightgown when she felt the cell phone in her pocket. It had been Tommy's, her grandson's, idea, the cell phone. In case Miriam fell, Tommy said, or something.

Miriam could imagine falling—on the back stairs, for example, where she sometimes forgot there were four steps instead of three. It was the *or something* that sometimes worried Miriam. She put it out of her mind or tried to, this nonspecific category of impending doom.

The phone was old-fashioned, but supposedly easier for senior citizens to operate. It felt heavy in Miriam's pocket. She opened it and punched the numbers.

The operator answered. What is your emergency?

For a minute, Miriam was confused. Her mind flashed to Alex Trebek, and the glare of the studio lights, and the way that everything was answered with questions. Miriam liked words and letters and before and after phrases. Bobby was the one who liked *Jeopardy!*.

Hello? the operator said. Are you hurt?

Earlier, when Miriam was in the street, she hadn't been able to move, and now she felt as though she couldn't speak. She tried hard, and something came out, and she couldn't have said later what it was, that she said, I lost Evie. Was something happening to her? Was she having a stroke?

Hey, are you okay?

In Miriam's mind, the words became like a chant, one of Evie's cheers. Hey, hey, are you okay?

Miriam felt the hand on her shoulder. She jumped at the touch, and some distant part of her expected to see her daughter there, not as Evie must look now, but as she had looked at seventeen, blonde hair in a tease, those big bright plastic earrings that Miriam had hated. Now, as Miriam had seen on TV and even at the grocery store, kids were piercing and tattooing every part of their bodies and the giant yellow circles that Evie hung from her ears didn't seem so bad. Miriam shouldn't have fussed the way she did. You're the one, Bobby had said during one of their discussions. You're the one who ran her off.

Evie, Miriam said, even though it wasn't Evie. She knew that. It was the girl from down the street. Ann was the girl's name. Ann something or other. Like always, Ann Something-or-Other was dressed in her overalls and her sunhat, and because Miriam herself liked to garden, she'd passed what was a not altogether generous judgment of Ann with her zinnias and her poor choice of roses and the beds that grew more weeds and grass than anything, and now that Ann was in front of her, now that Ann was so clearly and distinctly not Evie, Miriam had the impression that Ann was playing some trick on her.

I'm fine, Miriam said.

I heard you, Ann said.

The operator was talking. Tell me what happened, she said. Tell me what hurts.

Everything, Miriam said, and though nothing had really happened to her, what she said finally, for the first time in a long time, seemed true and right. She closed her eyes and opened them again, and the edges of things seemed sharper. From here, she could see Pete. She could see his tail whipping. My cat, she said. He's stuck on a pole.

≈

First came the police and then a fire truck and then a second fire truck. Over again, Miriam told the story of what happened. The paper should have been thrown onto her porch, but instead, it was thrown out into the street. That's how they did it now. That's where the world was. And she'd had to go get it. Pete—

And here, the cop stopped her. The cat? he said. Pete is the cat. Is that correct?

Miriam nodded. Pete had followed part of the way, and Spikey—

She paused, waiting to confirm that Spikey was the dog, but the cop said nothing, so Miriam went on. Spikey is never out of the fence.

Never say never, the cop said. He grinned and then caught himself. Then?

And then, Miriam said. This part was hazy, but she didn't tell the cop so.

Don't you know? Bobby had said. You have to be careful what you tell the police.

But Miriam hadn't known, and she'd told the cops that Evie's birthday was coming up. She'll be eighteen, Miriam said, thinking she was providing information, thinking she wanted to be as helpful as possible. Bobby told her later she should have kept her mouth shut because the police hadn't looked so hard after that. Evie wasn't a missing person so much as a girl who'd left home a few weeks early.

And then, Miriam said, Spikey got Pete in his mouth, but Pete got loose and ran up the pole, and now there they were. Pete was hurt. She was sure of it.

There was a whine to her voice and even to her own ears, Miriam seemed to move quickly and unexpectedly from patience to hysterics.

The cop closed his notebook and said something into his radio that Miriam didn't catch. His name was Officer Marty, and he went over to Spikey. He was scratching him behind the ears, and somebody had filled a paper picnic bowl with water.

Another car drove up. It was the fire chief, who, Officer Marty said, had been down to Waffle House with his wife and oldest boy. He pushed himself out of the SUV that belonged to the fire department. He took one look at the pole and said, There's nothing we can do about this. You'll have to call Duke.

Pete, it seemed, was perilously close to a transformer, and the fire department couldn't get up to the top of the pole without possibly electrocuting themselves. It wasn't a risk they were willing to take. Not for a cat, the chief said.

He's not just a cat, Miriam said.

Right, the chief said. I get it.

But Miriam knew he didn't. He didn't get it at all.

They were waiting on Duke Energy, and there wasn't much they could do but watch. All of them, even the fire chief, looked skyward, and they did their best to seem concerned even though many of them weren't, and if a stranger had come upon that scene and did not know there was a cat on the top of the pole, they might feel a certain shudder, the tremor of fear inspired by an unexpected astrological event. Miriam and the people there on the street looked to be staring up at the sky, as puzzled as an ancient tribe witnessing some imminent catastrophe they were too small, too weak, too stupid to stop.

And, in fact, there was some threat of explosion. If Pete—any part of Pete, including the bushy tail that curled and twitched—touched the transformer, he would be as good as gone. A regular firework show, the fire chief said under his sausage breath. His oldest boy, nine years old, giggled and hooked his thumbs in the waistband of his jeans to loosen them some.

Miriam made a low whining sound, and Officer Marty looked at the transistor and Pete up above it and said to Ann, Can you take her inside?

Ann reached out to Miriam, and again Miriam pulled away, but she wasn't so frightened this time. She just wanted to be left alone.

Miriam, Ann said, you think you could get me some water? I've been out in the yard all morning.

Miriam looked at the girl in the ridiculous hat and the overalls. It seemed more like a costume than anything anybody would really wear, and just seeing the girl made Miriam's head ache. I've got some orange juice, she said, and she let Ann take her arm. She let herself be guided back into her own house.

The day was already bright. Inside, it seemed strangely dark, and even though it was Miriam's house, the same house she'd spent most of her life, she found herself feeling her way along, using the edge of the kitchen counter to orient herself. Perhaps because it was so dark, the smell of things was even stronger.

Tomorrow, there was to be a visiting pastor at St. Matthew's where Miriam was a late-in-life member. She'd never been particularly religious and preferred to think of herself as educated and vaguely spiritual, but after Bobby died, Miriam realized that church served many purposes that didn't involve religion. Church, in part, kept old widowed women, like herself and like Clarice Powell and like so many women in Black Creek, from going completely crazy. It was a place you could at least see other people, talk to somebody if you felt like it.

Sometimes Miriam had trouble sleeping. She'd gotten up early that morning and started the pasta salad. It wasn't anything special. Just some roasted tomatoes and olive oil and basil, but everyone went on about it. They'd asked her to make it special for the pastor, and so she'd been about to roast the tomatoes when she felt a little flush, a little dizzy, if she were honest, and she'd gone outside to sit on the porch and get some air when she saw the Datsun and then the newspaper land square in the street. There were the tomatoes, sliced on the cookie sheet, a tin of brownies and a plate of tortilla roll-ups under Saran wrap and waiting on the counter. The kitchen smelled of cream cheese, salsa, and cocoa. Like, Miriam thought now, a holiday.

Outside, one of the police radios squawked. Someone, the chief's son maybe, laughed out loud.

You've been cooking, Ann said.

I have, Miriam said, and she didn't know whether it was the fact that Ann seemed to have a special way of stating the obvious—Sure is hot, Ann would say when Miriam passed by the house—or whether the events of the day had finally caught up to her, but she suddenly felt very tired. She'd forgotten she was still holding the paper. She turned loose of it, set it there on the table.

Ann was watching Miriam, but her eyes fell on the newspaper, the picture of the girls and their crowns. Look at them, Ann said. They don't know anything about anything.

It was a strange thing to say. Ann turned her back to Miriam and reached for the cabinets. Cups? she said.

Right. The girl had wanted some orange juice. I'll get it, Miriam said, and even though she was suddenly exhausted, she dragged over to the refrigerator and got the orange juice. She took down a glass and filled it from the jug.

When she turned around, Ann was sitting down at the table. The girl lowered herself gingerly as if some part of her was tender. She was too young for that, Miriam thought. Too young for the chronic pain that plagued Miriam and the other women at church. Miriam blinked, her eyes adjusting to the light. She watched Ann take off the hat and lay it on the table. Ann's bobbed hair was thin and stuck down on her forehead, which was paler, Miriam thought, than it should have been. Miriam was tired, but somehow Ann seemed even more worn out.

Miriam set the glass of orange juice on the table. Then she pushed it closer to Ann. I made some brownies, she said. Let me cut you a square.

Ann held up her hand. Her fingers trembled. That's all right.

But Miriam already had two plates out of the dish drainer. She peeled back the tin foil and cut a couple of generous portions. It was the kind of thing she and Evie used to do, after school when Evie was very little, before everything went so bad, when the biggest challenge they faced was the next day's spelling test.

You don't have to do all this, Ann said.

Miriam shook her head. She'd been too hard on the girl. What exactly did she want from people? It was something Bobby liked to ask her.

I didn't mean—Miriam started and stopped.

Ann held the glass. She pressed it to her forehead.

Miriam pulled out a chair and sat down in it. I didn't mean to get so upset, she said.

Ann smiled a quick smile. It's all right. She took a long drink that worked the chords in her neck. Then she set the glass on the table, but she didn't let go of it. Pets, she said.

Miriam nodded.

They're just like kids.

Yeah. She thought about Pete, the way he curled up in her lap. She took a bite of the brownie and tried to swallow.

What I'm saying is, Ann said, and she hesitated long enough for Miriam to look up at her. I'm saying that we can love animals like they're people, like children.

The girl went on, each sentence more complicated, more difficult to follow than the last. She was working through her own thoughts even as she spoke, and though some of it sounded like the sort of idle talk—Sure is hot. Think it'll rain?—that drove Miriam crazy, there was more to it than that. Ann was really looking for some kind of answer, a solution when Miriam couldn't follow the length of the problem. There was a certain gleam in Ann's eye, a sheen that bordered on the kind of hysteria that Miriam herself often felt but managed, she thought, to push down under the surface of things until it was nothing more than a hum any reasonable person could learn to ignore. All that stuff with Evie and Bobby—it all happened so long ago.

We're animals too, Ann said, when you get down to it.

Miriam swallowed, and time sort of stretched out between them so that the specifics of Ann's imploring mattered less than the urgency of her doubt, and Miriam might have told her then what it was like to have your daughter go missing, to be told a body had been found. She might have done her best to describe the wash of relief but also disappointment when that woman, a cop, called back to say the body wasn't Evie's after all. Miriam had been hopeful that at least a body would mean an end. Several years later, there had been a different kind of closure. Like something out of her shows, Miriam had hired an investigator. He'd found Evie only to determine that Evie hadn't gone missing but had run away. She had no real desire to ever come back for reasons Miriam didn't completely understand. Miriam could have done a little less fussing, like Bobby said, and there had been a thing about a boy Evie liked, but was this all it took? Was it true that the bond between them could be broken so easily?

I have a daughter about your age, Miriam could have said because just then she was beginning to sense that Ann had also lost something, and with this came the glimmer of recognition that if Miriam had misunderstood Ann, perhaps there were other things she wasn't seeing so clearly.

In that brief moment in the dark kitchen, so much moved between Miriam and Ann that the knock on the screen door caused them both to jump back as if they'd gathered around something that carried a charge and, losing themselves, gotten too close.

Miriam stammered. She hadn't forgotten about Pete on the pole. Of course she hadn't, but sitting there with Ann, she'd felt some distance from it.

There was the knocking at the door, and the shadow was short and wide, and for a minute, Miriam thought it was the fire chief, but when the door opened before she or Ann could move, Miriam saw that it was Cathy.

Inside the kitchen, Cathy seemed much larger. They told me what happened, she said.

A powerful force had passed through Miriam, and now she felt as though she was reeling herself back to the here, back to the now. What she said might have been a recording: Spikey's never out. Pete's hurt. Where were you?

Cathy rubbed a wide hand over the top of her buzzed head. We're installing a system. Security, she said. There's some boxes back there, and I think he jumped on them and got over the fence.

My husband says we should get a dog, Ann said.

Cathy turned. She seemed to see Ann for the first time. She stuck out her hand.

Ann just blinked. I've seen you with Spikey, she said. And the girl.

There was a look on Ann's face that was almost a smile, but her voice was sharper now. With Miriam, she seemed unsure of herself. But as soon as Cathy showed up, there was a kind of hardness about Ann, the same sort of tension Miriam had seen in Spikey just before he leapt at Pete.

It calms her down some, Cathy said. She talked about the baby, how they could hardly sleep at night, how the walking seemed to wear the girl out.

I knocked on your door, Miriam said.

I know it. They told me.

Miriam let out a little breath of air. She glanced at Ann, but Ann was staring hard at Cathy.

Did they tell you what happens when people's dogs get loose? Ann said. I bet they didn't tell you what they do.

Cathy didn't answer, and Miriam looked back and forth between them. They won't hurt Spikey, Miriam said.

It was a question really, but Ann didn't answer and finally Cathy turned away. She looked out the storm door and scratched at the back of her leg where there was a large tattoo of Caduceus—the staff and the snakes—inked in rainbow colors.

Now the news is here, Cathy said.

You're kidding, Miriam said just as the van pulled up and scraped the curb. On the driver's door was a magnetic sticker that said *The Record*.

They just want us to look bad, Cathy said. We're just trying to do our jobs.

At the moment, Cathy wasn't technically trying to do anything, but Miriam knew from previous conversations that as an EMT, Cathy considered herself of a kind with the fire chief, the police, and more broadly, the FBI and the FDNY. If one of them was on the job, all of them were.

Miriam looked down at the paper, wrinkled as it was from her grip. She felt oddly attached to it, as if the words on the page represented some part of her life that made a lot more sense. They're not so bad, she said.

All they do is talk bad, Cathy said. She coughed and cleared her throat, and it looked like she might spit right there on Miriam's floor, but she didn't. Criticize.

Maybe, Miriam said, but everybody knows better.

Miriam kept talking.

One time, I locked Tommy up in the car.

She told them Tommy was her grandson, that he'd come to visit her one summer. It had happened after they'd found out that Evie was living in Arizona, just outside of Flagstaff. And she had a little boy. Miriam hadn't thought about that day in years, but her mind was working in strange directions, and she felt a sudden and pressing need to say something in the dark kitchen that smelled now not so much like a holiday but a funeral.

This was years ago, she said. I was keeping him for—she stopped and started again. For a while. We were getting something or other at the store. Ice cream. Chips. This was before you had to put kids in the back, so he was in the front, and I threw my keys up on the dash so I could get him buckled in his car seat, and then I just locked and closed the door.

You left him in the car? Ann said. You just forgot?

Ann was doing more than trying to get the story straight. She seemed shocked at what Miriam had done, angry even. For the first time that day, Miriam saw some color in Ann's cheeks.

I didn't just leave him, Miriam said.

It happens, Cathy said. She rubbed at her face, at the dark circles under her eyes. Sometimes you mess up.

I didn't know what to do, Miriam said, so I called the police. They said they didn't handle unlocking doors, and I said, Even when there's a baby inside? Boy, they came then. I mean, they were there in minutes.

Even a few minutes is too long, Ann said, for a kid in a car.

We do our best, Cathy said. She gave Ann a hard look, but Miriam didn't notice.

Tommy was just laughing and pointing at the flashing lights and all. He loved every minute of it.

Ann shook her head. She put on her hat, pulled it tight down on her head, but she didn't get up.

It was just a photo and a caption—Baby Rescued! Then another time, I called up there to make sure they didn't print Bobby's obituary.

Miriam didn't know why she was talking or how one thing led to another.

I didn't know you could do that, Cathy said, not have an obituary.

If it's a baby, they don't make you, Ann said.

Miriam looked over at Ann, and a second later, so did Cathy. Ann's eyes went flat, and then she grabbed the paper. She bent her head so that the hat covered most of her face. Her fingers splayed over the big picture, those three young queens in glitter gowns, figures from a fairy tale.

Well, Miriam said. She'd felt a certain warmth in telling the story about locking Tommy up in the car. She'd remembered Tommy as a baby and herself younger and even though she did silly things like locking the keys in the car, she was strong and capable then. Back then, she hadn't thought about her time with Tommy as an opportunity to somehow set things right with Evie, though probably that's what she'd been doing. She was just glad that Evie had agreed to let Tommy come stay with her for a while. Miriam had felt good talking about it, but now she couldn't remember why she'd told that story in the first place. It seemed stupid.

It wasn't me that didn't want the obituary, she said. It was Bobby.

Bobby hadn't wanted a funeral either. What was a funeral anyway, he said, but a bunch of people sitting around eating and talking?

The preacher had said it was a bad idea, that the funeral really didn't have much to do with Bobby at all. That a funeral would give Miriam some chance at comfort, at peace.

At the time, though, Miriam had been intent on doing what Bobby wanted, no matter what it meant for her. He'd always blamed her for what happened with Evie, and this was something she could do to make it up to him.

Tommy was in the middle of a college semester three states away. Miriam tried to get in touch with Evie, but her address book included six different numbers for her daughter and all of them had been disconnected.

So that day at the cemetery, it had just been her and the preacher and a man in a backhoe waiting on the rise, and when it was over, Miriam came home and fell into the loveseat and Pete jumped up in her lap and together, they watched *Columbo*, and when she woke up, it was the next day. The TV was still on, and she was still in her funeral clothes, so nothing had changed, but everything was different.

They'll kill him, Ann said. They'll put him to sleep.

There was a part of Miriam that wasn't aware she was still sitting in the kitchen with Cathy and Ann, that she was holding the fork, that she was actually gripping it like a knife and refusing to let go. Miriam didn't realize that Tommy had come in either, that he was trying to take the fork from her, that he was saying, Mamaw, what happened?

There he goes! Ann shrieked. She jumped up from the table and pointed out the door, and Miriam turned just in time to see a flash of Pete across the yard.

Is he hurt? Miriam said, and they all—Cathy, Ann, Tommy, and lastly, Miriam—came tumbling from the house. They ran after Pete, toward the back fence, and although Miriam was old enough to be their mother or their grandmother, they were all as wild as children set loose on the world.

Pete was all right. He was down from the pole.

Miriam must have slipped out of her sandals because under her feet, the grass felt cool and pleasantly sharp. Some of the buttons on her nightgown had come undone, and her hand went up to her bare throat and felt a quick and hard pulse.

Along the back fence and now creeping closer to the house, there had grown all manner of strangling vines and privet. Miriam always kept her yard tidy, but she wasn't able to stay up on things as she used to. She hadn't noticed how bad things were until now. Her heart was pounding. She called out to the cat. Her voice was something like a howl.

≈

But Pete got away from them. They couldn't find him that day or the next or the day after that. *The Record* came out, and Tommy bought a copy so they could read the story. As it happened, there wasn't much of an article. It was about like the caption they'd ran about Tommy as a baby. Just two pictures—one of Pete on the top of the electric pole and another that wasn't Pete at all but another orange cat with much shorter hair. *Happy Ending!* the caption read. *Neighborhood cat saved by Duke Energy.*

Miriam stared at the pictures. So much had happened that day. So much had been said. It made her feel funny to see the imposter cat, as if she was the one who'd told a lie.

They were sitting on the front porch. Tommy shook out a cigarette and lit it. He looked at his phone.

He'd graduated college in May, and now he was, he said, planning his next move. Sometimes he came to see Miriam, but mostly he stayed with his friend, and there were girls, too. Miriam had seen Tommy eyeing Clarice Powell's granddaughter and another neighborhood girl she ran with.

When Miriam asked about Evie, Tommy said she still lived in Arizona. She had her own life. She was the same, whatever that meant.

Miriam stared at the newspaper, at the fuzzy pictures of the cats. Pete had jumped off the top of the electric pole. Miriam thought about the man in the truck. It's in their nature to be tough, he'd said.

How do you think they got that baby? she said. Cathy and her friend.

Tommy made a snorting sound. His thumb worked the buttons on the phone.

Two women, Miriam said. She'd only been mildly curious before, but the details seemed more important now. You think they used a turkey baster?

For once, Tommy looked up at her.

I'm just asking, Miriam said. It's good to ask.

Tommy shook his head and went back to his phone.

There's a lot we don't know, Miriam said.

Sure, Tommy said, though it was unclear what exactly he was answering.

They say it's not good for kids to have two men or two women for parents, Miriam said. She was looking out across the yard that needed cutting. She knew Tommy wasn't listening, but it didn't matter.

She was thinking about Cathy and her friend and the fence Spikey jumped. She was thinking about *Columbo*. About how she'd never been more scared in her life just sitting there in her own living room watching television. Her daughter was alive, and her husband was dead, but the truth was, she'd lost both of them a long time ago. Other than Tommy and the ladies at the church, Miriam was completely alone.

She was about to ask Tommy if he remembered that day in the parking lot when she'd locked him in the car. She was about to ask, even though he kept on laughing and gurgling and flailing as usual, did he feel the least bit scared? Was there ever a moment when he thought he might not be okay?

She was about to ask Tommy these questions, when under the wire fence, slipped a burred and muddy Pete.

Tommy didn't look up when Miriam stood and walked to the edge of the porch. He didn't see when she took the steps—four, not three.

Pete was running toward her. Miriam hadn't wanted to say so that day in the kitchen, but she knew it wasn't true— what Ann had said. In most ways, animals weren't anything like people.

But then, just when Miriam was close enough to touch him, Pete stopped short. His body went stiff and his eyes— Miriam could see the pupils go wide and flat. He wasn't hurt. He was scared. Something had happened to him. So much had happened to all of them, and it didn't matter that you tried to be careful, that you taught your animals to walk on leashes, that you built fences to keep certain things in and certain things out. Miriam saw that now. She understood the real dangers of the world, and all she could do was bend her knees and let things spin. All any of them could do was hold out their hands even as they showed their teeth.

FIRST-TIME USERS

Bev deserved more in life than an inflatable kiddy pool, but this, along with some ground round and a pack of butter buns, was the best Cathy and the Black Creek Dollar General had to offer.

Cathy was just off work from the Quick Stop. The cops who came in for coffee and peanuts said it was gonna be a long one. Crime went up with the temperature. In the summer, you could always expect domestics and a lot of 'em. Folks started sweating, and then they started drinking, and before you knew it, they were just tearing into each other. Heat like this, the fat cop said, makes people wild. Dumb and desperate.

Cathy's shoes stuck to the parking lot, and inside the car, the air was thick and hit like the flat of a hand.

On the ride home, Cathy wondered what she might be coming home to—Bev with her head under the faucet. Bev standing in the open icebox with her shirt pulled up over her bra. Or maybe Bev would be naked and asleep in a cold bath with ice cubes floating around her knees.

Cathy had seen all of these things before, and it was more disturbing than a person might think. Cathy couldn't shake the feeling that she was walking in on something she wasn't supposed to see. I can't remember a time, Bev said, when I wasn't burning up.

But this time, there wasn't anything to see. Bev's car was gone. There was a note on the counter. *Mozelle in bad shape. Be back late. Don't forget trash.*

Mozelle was one of Bev's residents. Bev bathed Mozelle and rolled her hair every day because Mozelle was sweet on another resident named Lewis who she sometimes took for her husband and other times thought was her father. She's eighty-four, Bev said, but she don't know it. Some days she thinks she's still a little girl.

Cathy knew Bev would be upset not if but when she lost Mozelle. Cathy didn't think it was good for Bev, that it would be good for anybody, to be around so much dying, but Bev said she was a professional. What was worse than sitting with a dying person was being that dying person and going it alone. Bev kept that from happening. She was the one who held hands and washed foreheads until the very end. She could handle it, she said. She had been handling it for nearly twenty years now, but Cathy wasn't so sure. Just because you kept living didn't mean you were okay.

Cathy still had the sack of groceries in her hand. She looked up from the note. There were some work trucks next door, but the engines and the hollers were muted by the windows and the blinds that were closed to the sun. The air conditioner kicked on. The fridge was running. Otherwise, the house was dark and quiet.

Cathy left Bev's note where she'd found it. She stuck the buns on top of the microwave. She took out the package of meat and opened the ice box. She was trying to decide whether to fridge it or freeze it. She saw the blood that ran and pooled at the corner of the deli Styrofoam.

Cathy and Bev had a lot in common. Sure they did. They both liked a good hamburger, for instance. But in some ways, they couldn't have been more different. Bev was used to blood, saw it all the time, but looking at the ground round, Cathy felt a lurching in her gut. She'd nearly been sick last week when Wally had a seizure and smashed his face against the ice cream freezer. Just before it happened, Cathy had asked where he'd left the mop. It was a simple question, but a certain look had come into Wally's eye, as if he saw through everything in front of him to an answer that was more complex than any of them could understand. The next thing Cathy knew, he was on the floor, trying to tear his clothes off.

Cathy hadn't ever had a seizure, but sometimes she felt like she was in a kind of daze. Snap out of it, Bev would say. Cathy blinked. She looked down at the ground round like she was just seeing it, and quickly, she shoved it into the freezer beside the Kool Pak Bev used for her migraines. There wouldn't be a barbecue that night, but she could have the pool set up by the time Bev got home. She wanted a surprise. She wanted to do something that day besides sell beer and cigarettes and lottery tickets. The pool would be good, Cathy thought. The pool would be something.

The box was small but heavy. Cathy carried it outside. She chose a spot where Bev used to set up her lawn chair before the headaches got so bad. The grass was crisping, and it was sharp, a kind of torture under Cathy's bare knees as she knelt to open the box.

Next door, Duke Energy was trimming branches off the line. There was the whining buzz of the chainsaw, the beep-beep of big things moving backward. A man yelled, Keep going!

Cathy had cooled some in the house, but already she was sweating again. She squinted against the sun. The pool was ten feet long and three rings. The box showed a father and mother, two kids, all Hispanic. The boy was throwing a beach ball. The girl was waiting to catch, her hands in the air.

But there was something unsettling about the picture that made it look like each person had been cut from another advertisement. Things were slightly out of proportion. The mother wasn't looking at the children. She was looking past them.

Cathy flipped the box over, pulled out her knife, and cut the tape. There was the strong odor of hot rubber.

That ain't level, a man said.

Cathy jerked around. She had the knife. She held it in front of her.

Whoa, the man said, and when he took off his hard hat, he caught Cathy's eye. She would have seen him before had she thought to look up about thirty feet where he stood in the bucket of a Duke Energy truck watching her. Whatever it is, he hollered down, I didn't do it.

Cathy held the knife. I'm innocent, the man said. He grinned with his mouth open until Cathy took the knife in her other hand. She folded it up, put it back in her pocket. But when she tilted her head back to see the man, she cocked an eyebrow so that her lip curled over her teeth.

The man put back on his hard hat. His hair was long and hung over his shoulders. Because of the sun, Cathy couldn't tell much else about him.

Just thought I'd tell you that what you're doing, the man said, it ain't gonna work.

The pool was still in the box. Cathy glanced at it. Then she said to the man, Hadn't done nothing yet.

Still. You'll need a straighter place.

Cathy studied the yard. It looked level enough from where she was, but maybe the man saw it different. She didn't like the way he was getting into her business, but it was true that from where he was, things were probably easier to see.

That side, the man said, pointing at Cathy. It'll cave right in, and then all your water—

He didn't say what the water would do. Instead he pushed his hands through the air, and his mouth puckered. In the sun, Cathy could see him spitting in the air.

I'm just warning you, he said. Those seams'll split.

Cathy looked at the house. You see somewhere better?

The man turned his head and reached for the controls. The bucket moved toward the house and back away from it. The mechanics of the machine were noisy, and the crane loomed like a giant version of the child's arcade. From such a vantage, the things over which the claw hovered were nothing but junk toys and cockeyed dolls. Because of their elusiveness and perhaps, too, their charming imperfections, they were the objects of sharpest desire, totems of the world's conditions contained so neatly within a lit glass box.

It's just a blow-up pool, Cathy yelled, but the man didn't hear her. The bucket moved, and the man surveyed the yard, and finally, he said, There's all right. He pointed at the spot where Bev usually parked her car, an oily patch of dirt in front of the shed.

Bev liked that spot because there was a tree and some afternoon shade, but the shade would be nice for the pool, too. And the man was right. The yard was more level there. All right then, Cathy said. She tilted her chin. Then she waved at him, but the bucket didn't move.

Appreciate it, Cathy said. She carried the box over to the spot in front of the shed. Still the man watched, and after a minute, after he'd watched Cathy wrestle the pool out of the box, he said, It's better with two people. Easier, I mean.

Cathy glanced up at him and went on unfolding the pool. She took out the manual, and when she opened it, carefully keeping her head down, she heard the gears of the bucket working. In the booklet, there were pictographs of a person diving, smashing her head against the bottom. The manual said every precaution should be taken. The manual said first-time users are at highest risk of incident.

You got a compressor? the man said, and the bucket had moved but not far.

Cathy looked up. Got a bike pump.

The man shook his head. Then he rubbed at his face. It was a gesture of real sadness, crushing defeat. You'll need a compressor, he said.

≈

For all his good advice, the man in the bucket didn't have much follow-through. Yeah, he had a compressor in the truck, but it wouldn't be smart of him to let Cathy use it. Company policy and all. What if something happened? I'd be glad to drop by, he said, after hours.

Cathy had short hair, and usually, this was enough. She wasn't used to men talking to her this way.

Think you got the wrong idea, she said.

The man in the bucket made a face and hitched a shoulder. Things aren't always how they look, he said. He watched her as he fired up the chainsaw. Then he turned and went at a limb.

The man was right. Cathy needed a compressor. Cathy pushed herself up, and for a strange minute—what was probably only a few seconds—she thought she might fall down. The burnt grass tilted and enough time passed for Cathy to think, This place isn't flat at all.

But then things snapped back and the yard held still. She left the pool laid out where it was in the yard. She locked up the house and got back in the car, which was nearly as hot as it had been earlier. She and Bev kept some tools in the hall closet—a hammer, nails, a dozen screwdrivers they'd bought as a set from Walmart. But Walmart was at the edge of town, and Cathy didn't feel like driving that far. The heat was working on her.

She pulled up to Higgin's Hardware. Besides the doors and the windows, the building was made entirely of corrugated metal and painted an ugly blue. When Cathy opened the glass door, a gust of conditioned air hit her face. It was as cool as the Quick Stop and felt good but made her head hurt, too.

Howdy, she said. Her eyes adjusted to the light, and she saw there was nobody at the register. It didn't seem like there was anybody in the whole store. There was a radio playing in the back, a song Cathy didn't know.

She took a few steps down the aisle. There were nails and screws, nuts and bolts. She'd never been inside Higgin's before, and she looked up for some sign of direction, but what she saw was taxidermy animals, most of them frozen and mounted in expression of struggle or attack. There were dozens of fish, curled as fish curl when they are out of the water and wanting more than anything to breathe. There were a couple of snarling hogs. A bobcat. Deer that looked serene but stupid, as if they'd been fooled and accepted it. And there, right on top of a shelf of motor oil, was a coiled up rattlesnake, its pink mouth open to strike.

Cathy reached out. She'd never been so close to a rattle-snake, dead or alive. Like needles, the fangs. A little pinch, Bev would say. Just a little pressure.

They'll kill you good, a voice said, and Cathy jumped to see a young man behind the other end of the counter. She hadn't seen him before, but he must have been there the whole time, leaning back in the chair like he was, chewing on a toothpick. It made her feel strange to think of him just sitting there watching her. All they need, he said, is half a chance.

Cathy looked back at the snake. Suddenly, it didn't seem so real. The eyes were poorly molded plastic, and the scales, even if they were real, seemed just as artificial. It was more like an imitation of itself, a piece of junk that had never been alive.

You killed it? Cathy said.

The boy didn't answer. He pointed up in the air. Shot that doe, he said, Thanksgiving weekend.

Cathy glanced up at the deer, at the ears which hung like a dog's.

The boy chewed the pick. You hunt?

Cathy shook her head.

You don't believe in it, the boy said. He didn't give her time to say whether she did or she didn't. There's hunting in the Bible.

Cathy scratched at her leg. Something had bit her. She felt the knife in her pocket. I'm looking, she said, for an air compressor.

It had been cool when she'd first walked in, but she was feeling the heat again, a damp run down her back. Cathy was looking around the store, but the boy kept his eyes on her. He said, Every living thing is made for us. For men, I mean.

Outside, a cloud passed before the sun, making the day seem suddenly later than it was. I need a compressor, Cathy said, so I can blow something up.

There's a compressor there, a woman said. She'd come from the back where the music was playing. She wiped her forehead with the back of her wrist, and there was dirt there like she'd been working. You got a flat?

I got a pool, Cathy said.

The woman didn't smile, but she came out from behind the counter. Lucky you, she said.

Yeah, lucky me.

The woman squatted. Her nametag said Jill. She took a box off the shelf and handed it to Cathy. This one ought to do it, she said.

Cathy looked at the box. All right.

You can hook it up to the car, Jill said. To the lighter.

Cathy nodded.

Jill stood up. She made her way to the register. She didn't look at the boy, but she talked at him. Boone, I thought you were supposed to be at some revival.

Boone eyed her with no small amount of meanness. Nope.

That it for you? Jill said, and Cathy told her that it was. Cathy said, I like your hair.

It wasn't something Cathy would normally say. Truth be told, she didn't usually say much to anybody. She kept things to herself and kept herself from other people. But there she was talking and sounding, she thought, pretty stupid.

The color of it, she stammered because Jill's hair was sort of streaked with a reddish-purple color, and even though her hands were dirty, her fingernails were polished that same bright plum.

I get it done, Jill said, in Columbia. I lived there for a while.

Cathy nodded. That's where you're from?

That's where I lived.

But now you're here, Boone said. He pointed at the ceiling. He knows best. He's got the plan.

Jill cut her eyes down the counter.

Everything happens for a reason, Boone said.

Shut up, Jill said. Nobody's listening to you.

They ought to. They ought to if they know what's good.

What's good is letting people live and leaving them alone.

You were alone. Look how that turned out.

Jill glared down the counter, but a muscle twitched under her eye. Something about that flinching put Cathy in mind of a lightning strike, the way the sky will light up just before it pours.

Boone here, Jill said, thinks he's gonna turn himself into a preacher.

And Jill thinks she's gonna turn herself into an angel.

Jill looked at Cathy. Sorry. She pressed a button on the register, told Cathy what she owed.

Cathy opened her checkbook and started writing. She didn't like the way the boy was talking, the way he stared at her. She needed to get back home. If she could just get the compressor and go.

Is there somebody helping you? Jill asked.

Cathy was writing the check, and for a minute, what Jill said was all tied up with numbers. It must have shown on her face because Jill said, With the pool.

Cathy looked at Jill, at the little scar just under the woman's eye. It was an old cut and wouldn't have been visible in some lights.

It goes quicker with two people, Jill said.

Cathy went back to the check. She signed her name, tore it out, handed it over. I've got time.

Jill took the check. Maybe it's on your side, she said and she looked at Boone, and it seemed to Cathy like she was trying to make a joke, but it was hard to say what, if anything, was funny.

≈

Cathy did what Jill said. That is, she drove up close to where she had the pool spread out across the dirt. She plugged the compressor into the lighter. She shoved the other end of the tube into the pool and flipped the switch.

Next door, they were still working on the trees, but the bucket truck was in another part of the yard, and Cathy could barely hear the saw over the roar of the compressor.

It was slow going, three rings, and each had to be filled separately. The instructions said to squeeze the base of the valve stem to open an internal check valve while inflating. Cathy sat on the ground and held the valve. She studied the pictures. They'd sprung for a real photograph on the outside of the box, but the manual only had drawings. A grown-up watching a child with what looked like, thanks to the lines following his sight, laser vision. This beside the cartoon of a person jumping head first and cracking her skull, a little explosion at the point of impact.

Cathy held the valve, and the motor ran, and she felt her eyes going dry. The muscles in her arm were hard knots.

Wally said people used to think epilepsy was some kind of religious experience. When you had a seizure, he said, they thought you saw God.

Cathy had been stocking the cigarettes, Seneca soft packs in particular. She'd been holding a pack. She'd been squeezing them so hard she could feel the cigarettes like bones, like fingers, like a hand she was holding. She asked Wally what happened when he had a seizure. She said, What do you see?

Wally put his hand in his hair, and when he pulled it back, his face seemed bigger, like he wasn't so far away, but then he was pulling his bangs down again. He was covering up one eye and most of the other in the way that he liked. Maybe I don't remember, he said.

When the first two rings were done, Cathy brought out the water hose and turned on the faucet. She wasn't sure if this was okay, to fill the pool with the water before she'd aired up the whole thing, but it was past six now. It was almost seven.

Cathy was holding the hose when the car pulled up, and before her mind could catch up, she thought it might be Bev.

But it wasn't. The car was blue instead of brown, and when Cathy squinted against the sun, she could see the driver, the red hair.

Jill cut the engine, got out of the car, and walked over to where Cathy was. Nice work, she said, and she had to yell to be heard over the compressor.

Part of Cathy was surprised to see Jill, but in ways Cathy couldn't explain, Jill being there didn't seem strange at all. The pool was holding water. The pool was perfectly level.

You've almost got it, Jill hollered.

Several minutes passed, and the compressor worked, and Cathy and Jill didn't talk at all. They just stood there looking down at the pool, at the air and the water that was slowly filling it. They studied as people study a river or a fire or anything that is bigger than them and moves of its own volition.

When the third ring was full of air, it was Jill who switched off the compressor, and because she was closer, because it was—as Jill and the man in the bucket said it would be—easier with two people—it was Jill who got in the Mountaineer and unplugged the compressor and backed up away from the pool and cut the engine. She moved with a kind of efficiency that suggested confidence and experience.

She got out and tossed the keys back to Cathy, and without the compressor, without the running engine, things were suddenly very quiet. Cathy listened for the saws but didn't hear them. She said, How'd you know where I lived?

The store, Jill said. The check.

Oh, right. She held the water hose. She moved it around even though she didn't need to. She felt the spray of it on her leg. Nobody writes checks anymore.

Jill rolled her shoulder. Sometimes we just want things to stay the same.

Cathy kept her head down, but she was watching Jill. She was studying that scar, more like a split Cathy saw now. I keep thinking about all those dead animals, Cathy said.

Don't ask me.

I thought you had to cut their heads off. Snakes.

Jill bent down and picked up the pool manual. You do, she said.

So they sew the head back on when they stuff it?

I guess. People do all sorts of things.

Cathy looked back at the water. The pool was almost full. Everybody's been trying to help, she said.

Jill kept her head down. She flipped to the drawings. Maybe you look like you need it.

Next door, a truck was backing up.

I don't know why, Cathy said.

Jill closed the manual. She stuck it under a rock to keep it from blowing anywhere. Good luck with the pool. And she was walking backward now. She was making her way toward her car. I think he got that snake off the internet. They probably made it in China.

Cathy looked up and said, Be careful! She meant the heat, the way it made people do things.

Jill stuck her hand up in the air. It was something you'd do if you were too far away, if someone couldn't hear you, but Cathy wasn't that far. She was just close enough.

≈

By eight that night, Bev still wasn't home. Maybe this time, Mozelle really was dying. There'd been scares in the past, but maybe this was it. When Cathy imagined it, when she looked at the pool but saw beyond it, she saw a head, severed and still snapping. The body a live wire.

She stood in the yard wearing Bev's red bathing suit. The material strained in the middle and hung loose in the nubby seat.

You better get in, the man said. He was still in the bucket, and he'd swung back around over the yard. It's getting late.

You're still working, Cathy said.

Yeah, the man said. Emergencies.

He stared down at her and said, Watch out for storms. Then the bucket moved up and around, and Cathy watched him go. Cathy watched until he was on the other side of the house and out of sight.

The water was colder than she expected, and she had to force herself to put both feet in, to sit down. She tried to relax like the family on the box. She was right about them, the way they were cut and pasted from elsewhere. No way could so many people fit in a space so small.

This was the time of year when even the nights were hot, and although the water did provide some relief, it was almost too much. Cathy shivered in it, as people do when they are cold or burned or especially afraid. Shock, the cops called it.

Tomorrow, she would get up and work the same shift. She would stock the cigarettes. She'd clean the tubes in the soda machine. She'd tell Bev she loved her.

Cathy looked down. She looked for herself in the water. She tried to see what everyone else saw, what she was missing.

She'd thought about being a fireman, maybe even a cop. She could be out there with them, eating peanuts and drinking coffee and generally keeping folks from killing each other. Maybe she could make some kind of difference. She and Wally had talked some about it. She'd said that someday she might like to do something different. She'd meant school and work but she'd meant other things, too, and Wally said, I'm just trying to make it. I'm just trying to stay alive.

But Wally was saving up for cosmetology school. He'd talked about doing makeup, maybe even masks for movies. There were people, he said, who did that.

There was just enough water in the pool. Just enough so that Cathy could float. She couldn't see herself. She couldn't see what she needed, but for the first time, she felt what wasn't there. If the man in the bucket were here now, if he were to look down at her, he would see that a person is shaped like a star. Maybe people, like stars, can be gone before anyone sees the flash, the pulse of distant collapse and subsequent release.

The sun was back behind the trees now, and because she was wet, Cathy was colder outside of the water than underneath it. She ducked under. She heard the sounds of the world as if they were so many miles away. She pressed her head against the bottom of the pool. She opened her mouth. When the skull is cracked or the head is severed, the body still moves as if by a current, as if by the same charge that, against the dark, creates one small point of light.

LIVING THINGS

L ewis and Mozelle were making finger whoopee again.
That's what Lewis told Bev, anyway. Bev didn't
know where he'd come up with this term, finger whoopee.
Maybe a relic from his own youth. It was too sweet, after all,
too innocent to have come from Natalie and the other girls.
Bev was sure they would call it something else, something
a lot nastier.

All right, Bev said. She yanked up the blinds. Then,
in that brightness, she pointed at Lewis and said, Get out
of here.

To his credit, Lewis tried to hustle, but he was slow in
sitting up, in pushing himself off the bed. He was eighty-
six years old. Mozelle was eighty-five. Both of them were
in their underwear, which because they were lying in bed
together, was against regulation. When Lewis bent over for
his pants, Bev saw the ugly scar on his leg. It looked like
something that would happen in a war, but Bev knew it was
from Lewis's hip replacement.

Mozelle pulled the thin sheet up around her chin. She
started to whimper. Sorry, she said over her bottom lip. We
didn't mean to.

Lewis fumbled with his zipper. Speak for yourself.

Lewis, Bev said, Please.

Lewis couldn't get a hold of the zipper pull. Bev watched
him grabbing at nothing. He said, She meant what she was
doing plenty enough a minute ago.

I'm sure she did.

You need a contract these days, a voice said. Signed, sealed, and delivered.

Bev knew Natalie's hoarse twang, heard it sometimes even when she wasn't at Twilight, but when Natalie came around the corner and into the room, it took Bev a minute to register the new hair, a dramatic red curl that Natalie pushed back with a long green fingernail.

Better ask for an ID, too, Natalie said, patting Lewis on the back. We don't want you getting yourself on the registry.

Natalie, Bev said.

Natalie bent to zip up Lewis's pants. Come on, Mr. Lewis. They're about to spin the big wheel.

Bev could hear the television in the day room, the announcer describing every detail of a brand new Harley Davidson. *Find your open road!* Then the indiscernible voices in the crowd. They could have been yelling about anything.

I've told you about those nails, Bev said. Natalie and Lewis were nearly out of the room, and Bev's words tumbled out in a rush. She meant to sound authoritative, but even to her own ears, there was the warble of panic. You'll scratch the residents, she yelled after them.

Natalie had Lewis by the elbow. I think somebody's winning big today, Natalie said. I feel it.

Mozelle's crying had gotten worse. She was breaking into all-out sobs. She and Bev were alone now. It's all right, Bev said. It's okay.

I didn't know what he was gonna do, Mozelle said. We were just going to the show.

I know. Let's get you cleaned up.

She helped Mozelle out of her bra and underwear and got her situated on the plastic stool they kept in the shower.

Natalie and the other girls used the orange antibacterial hand soap for baths, for shampooing, for everything, and they didn't seem to notice how it dried out the skin. Bev, though, brought her own shower kit, and soon the air smelled like vanilla.

Mozelle did some of the work, and Bev helped her wash the soap from under her arms and breasts. When Bev first started this job, nearly twenty years ago, she felt a little uncomfortable with the exposure, the touching, the intimacy. But it didn't bother her anymore. She didn't really think about it. Even bathing herself had become a chore, something like washing a dog or a car.

When it was done, Bev turned off the water and helped Mozelle stand up. Slow down. Easy, she said, she always said, as Mozelle took that dangerous step from the ceramic tile to the rug.

Mozelle kept her balance. Water dripped from her hair and down her face. She licked it from her lips, and if she was still crying, Bev couldn't tell. With the towel, Bev wiped Mozelle's face first and then worked her way down. She was careful not to press too hard. An old person's skin was like paper and any old thing could cause Mozelle to bleed.

Smells good, Mozelle said. Like birthday cake.

Bev smiled. She was drying Mozelle's feet now. She noticed fungus growing around Mozelle's big toe. It's got a silly name, Bev said. She meant the soap. A Thousand Wishes it's called. Isn't that stupid?

A Thousand Wishes, Mozelle said.

Here you go, Bev said. She held out a fresh pair of blue underwear.

Mozelle braced herself and stepped in one hole and then the other. Bev pulled up the elastic band and made sure it wasn't twisted around Mozelle's waist, which was still amazingly narrow. Mozelle had been Miss Sweet Potato 1952. She kept a photo of herself by her bed. There she was in her crown and sash, her very own sweetheart.

I'd settle for one wish, Mozelle said.

Oh yeah? Bev buttoned Mozelle's shirt. It was a lightweight denim poorly painted with lopsided jack-o-lanterns and black blobs meant to be cats with their hair standing on end. It came in the mail for Mozelle, a gift from a granddaughter she'd never met.

Mozelle closed her eyes like she was praying, and she said, I wish me and Henry would have gone to see that monkey like we were supposed to. I wish we hadn't done what we done.

That sounds like two wishes, Bev said.

Mozelle opened her eyes. She looked straight at Bev. For a minute, there was no sound at all save for the television in the other room, and there with them, the showerhead leaking. Bev thought Mozelle would say something, but instead, Mozelle took a deep breath and blew in Bev's face, as if what she saw was the smallest of flames, a lick of fire that twisted and flickered before it would go out completely.

≈

Later, at the front desk, Natalie and another girl, Trish, were filing their nails and flipping through a magazine. It was true that for some, the job came with a lot of down time, but Bev always found something else to do: a form to fill, a pan to empty, a gown to change. Her mother said she had busy hands. Busy hands, Bev said and repeated, a mantra to anyone that was around. Busy hands made the day go faster, but no one ever agreed or said otherwise. It seemed like no one was ever really listening.

Natalie and Trish were talking about a new music video they'd seen, a rapper with a name Bev didn't catch.

That one girl, Natalie said, on the car?

Total skank, Trish said and turned the page. Hoe if I say so.

People were always bringing magazines to Twilight. Sometimes there were boxes stacked taller than Bev outside the door. They must have thought that's all the old people did—sit around looking at *Popular Mechanics* and *Sports Illustrated* and *OK!* As if being in a nursing home was like waiting in a permanent doctor's office. But really, the residents hardly ever looked at the magazines. The girls looked at them, and then their kids cut them up for art projects. Trish's son was working his way through twelve years of *National Geographic*. Trish said he was going to be a scientist.

But Baby D, Natalie said, he's looking good!

Know what I'm saying? Trish said, and she thrust her hips back and forth so that the chair rolled against the counter. She and Natalie doubled over laughing, and then they saw that Bev was watching.

Trish looked back down at the magazine, but Natalie said, That's your problem, Bev. You don't have enough Baby D in your life.

Bev held her pen with both hands like she was afraid somebody was after every little thing she had. What's Baby D?

Trish snorted.

Danger, Natalie said like it was obvious.

And love, Trish said.

Well, Natalie said, not love exactly.

Then what exactly? Bev whined.

That was the truth. While everyone else was laughing, Bev was whining. Bev felt like she didn't know what people were saying anymore. She couldn't follow the track of things, but it didn't matter. The girls were already on to something else.

They were talking about Iva, a resident who apparently had a full-blown orgasm during physical therapy.

I said get her up off that table, Natalie said. Let that therapist put his magic hands on me.

Bev felt a rising heat coming up from her neck. She often broke out in hives, great red splotches that caught people's attention. She lowered her chin, pulled at the collar of her shirt.

It was getting toward midday. Lunch would be soon. In the dayroom, the game shows had faded into soap operas. It was the men who really dialed in to *Young and the Restless* and especially *Days of Our Lives*. The women all nodded off or stared out the big glass door as if they'd had enough romantic drama for one lifetime.

≈

After work, Bev went to the Walmart. She needed—what? Lightbulbs and a sack of frozen broccoli.

Driving out to the bypass, she was overwhelmed by the realization that these items were on opposite ends of the store. Work hadn't been especially taxing, but lately, Bev was always exhausted. She felt like she never had the energy to do anything anymore. Her roots were showing, for example, and she'd have liked some new, bigger pants, but when

she thought of putting on the gloves for the hair dye or going to the store to try on slacks, she just wanted to pull her
hair back, put on a pair of sweats, and lie down on the couch
with a bag of Doritos and a jar of peanut butter. Maybe, she
thought, this was what getting old was like.

A couple of months ago, Bev's mother had died. It wasn't
unexpected. Her mom was sick for some time, lymphoma
that was there and went away and then came back again.
Bev's father had been dead for nearly ten years now. At Twilight, Bev saw people die all the time. She hadn't expected
to take her mother's passing so hard, but maybe she had.
Something, at least, was bothering her.

Bev's girlfriend, Cathy, said that a period of mild depression was a completely natural response to the death of
a loved one. Cathy had decided that she wanted to become
a paramedic. Last summer, she'd bought an inflatable pool,
and it was possible, Cathy said, for a kid to wander up, jump
in, and drown.

It only takes a few inches, Cathy said, and there was, in
Cathy's voice, a desperation so pronounced that Bev had
to remind herself they were talking about the hypothetical
drowning of an imaginary child. I wouldn't even know what
to do, Cathy said, and by August, she had enrolled in some
courses at Tech. Her favorite class so far was psychology.
Now that pool was a flat piece of rubber moldering in the
yard.

Bev pulled into the parking lot, which stretched into a
terrifying expanse of asphalt. The Walmart was only a couple of years old. When they built it, they had to push down
a square mile of pine and a bamboo grove. In the place of
these old trees, they set in some maples, which were still so
spindly, they had to be held up with ropes.

Bev got out of the car and locked the doors. She was crossing over toward the store when she passed a woman in a Redskins sweatshirt. The woman had drawn-on eyebrows and seemed vaguely familiar. A resident's daughter, maybe?

How are you? the lady said.

Fine, fine, Bev said, and even though she thought she knew the woman, she kept walking. Really, Bev didn't feel fine. Really, she didn't feel any better than those dying, propped-up maples.

She passed through the automatic doors and headed toward the hardware section. Walmart was nearly more than Bev could handle, but there was also something thrilling about it. There was, in that place, everything a person would need to make her life better. Coffee makers that brewed one cup at a time or a whole pot. Lotions that filled in and eventually removed wrinkles. Wax cubes that promised to make your house smell like *that perfect fall sky*. The combination of excitement and terror was something like riding a roller coaster, which Bev hadn't done since she was a teenager and couldn't imagine doing now.

Her heart pounded, and her mouth went dry. She grabbed a Diet Mountain Dew out of the fridge by the checkout lines. You weren't supposed to open drinks in the store, but she did it anyway. Sue me, she said to no one. She took a long drink and belched.

Later, she would think about going to the store, and she'd have trouble remembering what all happened and in what order. Under those bright lights, with the distant chime of the register, things seemed possible. It seemed possible, for example, that you could buy enough of all the right things to transform yourself, and isn't that what Bev wanted? Some kind of transformation? That feeling the girls were talking about?

Music played from the ceiling, and Bev wondered if this was Baby D. She'd been so tired earlier, but now, as she listened to the beat, to the unbelievable rush of the lyrics, she was experiencing a surge of energy. She was headed back to the hardware section for lightbulbs, when a display in the center of the aisle caught her attention.

Bev could feel her eyes moving in their sockets. She could feel a pulse in her throat. The EastPoint Fold 'N Store Table Tennis Table. *Sets up in minutes!* the box said. *So small, you can do whatever works for you!*

She took another slug from the bottle. There was caffeine in that drink, to be sure, but what Bev was experiencing was stronger than that. The urgency she felt came from a deeper place, the part of Bev that dared to hope for something more than what she saw in the world, something more than what she felt, more than she herself was.

She screwed the cap back on and took hold of one of the boxes. It was heavier than she thought, and she wouldn't be able to get the other things she'd come for, but that stuff didn't really matter. Broccoli. How stupid! What mattered just then, what was absolutely essential for reasons Bev would have had a hard time explaining, was something out of the ordinary, was dragging this box halfway across the giant store. *Sets up in minutes!* she read as she heaved and shoved. *Whatever works for you!*

Need some help? a man said. He didn't work there. He was just a man.

Bev shook her head. Nope, she said. I got it. I got it now for sure.

≈

When Bev unlocked and opened the front door, Cathy was on the couch under a pile of books and papers. She had the TV tray set up in front of her, and there were more books on top of that, and on top of everything was a spiral notebook in which Cathy seemed to always be scribbling very important notes.

Here I am, Bev said.

Yeah, Cathy said, and she moved her head, but her eyes stayed on the paper. She continued to write. Did you get the stir-fry stuff?

Bev felt strange, like some integral part of her face had sprung loose. I got something else, Bev said. She stood in the door, which was still open. Come see.

Cathy kept writing. Just a minute, she said. She was talking to herself.

Bev blinked and touched her temple where there was the beginning of a terrible headache. What? she said. What are you saying?

Prions, Cathy said. Misshapen strands of protein that cause neighboring proteins to bend out of shape.

Oh, Bev said. Yeah.

Bev had taken science classes for her CNA, but she didn't remember whatever word it was that Cathy was saying.

Come on, Bev said. It was a surprise, and she was trying to sound excited. She was trying to feel what she'd felt, what she thought she'd felt, in the store, but the exhaustion was creeping back. Her head was really hurting.

Finally, Cathy got up and made her way to the door. Together, they went out to the car and Bev popped the trunk, and she might have been revealing a dead body for all the enthusiasm Cathy showed. Ping-Pong? she said.

It's not Ping-Pong, Bev said, and there was the whine again. It's—she read the box, she pointed to each word—an EastPoint Fold 'N Store Table Tennis Table.

Cathy crossed her arms. She looked at Bev. Ping-Pong, she said.

It's different, Bev said. I think it's different.

Bev stared at the man on the box. He had black hair and incredibly white teeth. He looked like a male Barbie. I thought it'd be fun. She squinted against the pain.

Your head.

It's okay. It's all right.

I'll get your Kool Pak, Cathy said. She wrestled the box out of the trunk.

I'm just tired.

Get one end? Cathy said. They took hold of the box. You're right. Cathy was trying. It'll be fun.

Cathy had one end, and Bev took the other, and, like pallbearers, they carried the box together.

Every Friday before Halloween, the fifth-grade class from Black Creek Elementary came to trick or treat at Twilight Nursing Home. It was one of those community outreach initiatives thought up by an ambitious first-year teacher who was no longer a teacher at all but instead worked as a part-time hairstylist who mainly just stood outside of the Klip and Kurl smoking Basic Menthol Light 100's. Still, the tradition was carried on by a group of haggard veteran teachers who, if nothing else, appreciated the chance to get out of the classroom.

They pushed the kids ahead, through the big glass doors and into the foyer that smelled like a nursing home, like coffee and white gravy and other things. And these boys and girls who had, that morning, been beyond excited to dress up as superheroes and magical fairies and glittery kitty cats were now petrified of what they were seeing—the masks which were really not masks at all but ancient human faces sneering in confusion, pain, or else in a desperate attempt at joy; yellowed claws reaching out to pinch fat cheeks; and there, too, was all manner of amputation and scar and removal of nonessential parts like noses and the tops of ears, places where cancer liked to bud and bloom.

A few kids actually turned and ran away, and they had to be corralled and sternly spoken to by the teachers. Imagine she's your grandmother, one teacher said. Imagine she's you eighty years from now.

Watching from the front desk, Bev wondered if there was something instinctual in the way the kids responded. She had a dog once that got into a pack of M&M's. He'd eaten the colored coating off all the candies but had left the chocolate. He seemed to know it would hurt him, just as these kids, so new to their own lives, seemed naturally repelled by those so late in theirs.

Yoohoo, Natalie was saying. Apparently, she'd been trying to get Bev's attention for some time and was now shaking Bev by the shoulder. You got that candy?

Sorry, Bev said, shaking her head. She reached under the desk. Yeah, here.

She handed over the candy they kept hidden. They couldn't trust the residents. Some would eat it all at once, and others would squirrel it away. Just the other day, they'd found forty-nine Shasta sodas hidden in a closet, and Lewis was real bad to hide bananas. Everywhere you looked— under the sofa cushion in the dayroom, on top of the tall cabinet in the PT room, even in the shower—there was a banana in various stages of rot and decay. Food hoarding was a common problem. It seemed like the residents were stocking up, preparing for something big. A major disaster, Bev thought. An apocalypse.

Reluctantly, the kids stepped up to the wheelchairs and held out their bags. Some of the residents dropped the candy like they were supposed to. Others just fiddled with the wrappers, then ate whatever was inside.

Mozelle stood apart from the others. She was holding something, a wadded towel. The hoarding. The finger whoopee. The issues with physical therapy. You couldn't put much past the residents. Mozelle might just be holding a towel, but the towel, Bev knew, could just as easily be covered in something like poop which would, Bev knew, not be good on a day like today, in front of the already scared children.

Bev came out from behind the desk and edged her way around the group until she was standing beside Mozelle. She was about to say something when Mozelle spoke first. You're not gonna make it, she said.

Bev jerked her head around. What?

I said I can't wait, Mozelle said. Her eyes were low, and she was rocking back on her heels. I can't wait, I can't wait, I can't wait.

When Mozelle and any of the other residents who suffered from dementia seemed confused, it was better just to play along. It's like dealing with a sleepwalker, Bev had explained to Natalie and the others. It's better not to wake them up. Over the years, Bev thought she'd perfected the kind of responses that avoided both agitation and contradiction.

I can't wait, Mozelle said.

You seem pretty good, Bev said. At waiting.

Mozelle went on. It'll be our turn soon. Mine and Lewis's. She looked back in the corner, where Lewis was slouched, dozing on the plaid couch. Beneath one of the pillows was the black tip of a banana.

Mozelle turned around to study the children. They're so young, she said.

Makes us even older, Bev said. She worked her lips into what was supposed to be a smile but wasn't exactly.

Maybe he'll be an astronaut, Mozelle said. She might have been talking about Lewis. She might have been talking about one of the little boys. She might have been talking about no one Bev could see. Like Neil Armstrong.

So when the world ends, Bev said, he can just put on his suit and get in the rocket and go someplace else.

This was not the right thing to say. Bev knew it but said it anyway. She was feeling the familiar ache deep in her mind. Headaches, Cathy said, were a common feature of depression. But this wasn't the regular dull throb. This was a hot and sudden popping.

Mozelle kept talking. Whatever he does, he'll be a hero.

Maybe *he* will be a *she*, Bev said. Mozelle reminded Bev of her own mother. In a way, this was a good thing, and in other ways, it most certainly wasn't. Just now Bev was grinding her teeth.

He can do anything he wants, Mozelle said. He has his whole life ahead of him. See?

Mozelle lowered the towel, cradled it out and away from her so Bev could see what she held, that what she held was nothing but the towel itself, and of course, it wasn't surprising—the fact of there being no baby—but what Bev felt in that moment was a greater kind of shock, a burst of tragic disappointment that was bigger than Mozelle, that was bigger than Bev, that was bigger than all of them.

There was, it seemed, for something so powerful, no more reasonable response than violence, and so in that second and the next, it was almost natural to Bev that her muscles would tense, that an arm with a fist would swing up and away from her side and toward Mozelle, toward everything that in that moment drew up such a fury. It was only normal to rage against the real and pure terrors of the world that Mozelle and the empty towel and Twilight itself seemed to gather and thrust at Bev until she shook, until she very nearly collapsed under the weight, the threat of it all. No child in that room was ever so afraid.

And so it seemed right and, in fact, predictable for Bev to finally fight back, for her to, at last, strike out at the myriad forces against her. What was not expected was the other hand, the stronger hand, and those sharp nails which pierced with precision and intent, and Natalie saying Miss Bev, and Natalie smiling, and Natalie catching Bev before it was too late. Natalie saving Mozelle from what would certainly have been a crushing blow. Natalie so sweetly asking Miss Bev to please get back to the desk, to please get the children some more candy before there was some kind of—ha, ha—trouble.

≈

What Bev needed, Natalie said, was a good vacation. She slid over a damp curled issue of *Country Living*. There was a picture of a woman, a blonde, with a basket on her arm. In this basket was a loaf of bread and a bottle of wine. A grinning man was beside her with a red-and-white checked blanket under his arm. He looked like the man on the table tennis box which still sat unopened in the middle of the living room floor. Bev had tripped over the box on her way to work that very morning. She read the magazine head-line. *You only live once!* Natalie stared and clacked her nails against the counter like she was waiting on something.

I've always wanted to go to Asheville, Bev said and said again at home that night with Cathy, and the second time she said it, she almost believed it. Asheville was mountains and pine trees and that day, when Bev should have been doing her paperwork, she'd read on the computer that there were even bears. She'd never seen a bear before, and she was pretty sure Cathy hadn't either. If they ended up spotting one, Bev was sure it would be magical—like see-ing Mount Rushmore or Niagara Falls, other things she hadn't done. There was so much.

She told Cathy they had to go. This weekend. Maybe she could take off Friday.

Cathy had a test coming up. There was no way she could go. She'd planned on studying.

But Bev looked so dejected, so utterly deflated, that Cathy finally relented. She'd take Bev somewhere if it was that important, but not to Asheville. She couldn't go to Asheville, but maybe they could go over to that new restaurant, what was it called? Ceiling? Shingle?

The restaurant was twenty minutes away, but it was away, and this was good, Bev thought. This was something.

She wore a flannel under a green sweater, and Cathy had on an FDNY T-shirt and a pair of men's cargo pants, and both of them seemed mightily underdressed for this place called Roof, which was—it turned out—a rooftop bar meant for what Bensburg called its young professionals.

Women wore heels, and the men had on jackets with embroidered pockets, and Bev and Cathy stuck out, Cathy said, like sore thumbs, but no one made a move to kick them out. So they ordered fruity mixed drinks and stayed.

It was cold. The building was only a couple of stories, but still, up here, the wind seemed to blow harder and from a different angle. Cathy's hair was very short, but Bev's whipped around her face, and she kept having to pull it out of her mouth.

I feel like I'm underwater, she said.

They drank their drinks, which tasted something like snow-cone syrup. Bev watched a couple near the edge of the roof. The man swirled his drink around and said something that made the woman laugh. She stepped out of one of her shoes, put her hand on his arm.

Isn't it dangerous, Bev said, to be so close to the edge?

But Cathy wasn't really listening. She'd pulled out her flash cards. She must have felt Bev watching her. What? she said. We're just sitting here.

Bev licked her lips. They were sticky from the drink.

Here, quiz me.

Bev took the cards. She opened her eyes wide. Then she squinted. What are, she read, the characteristics that distinguish living things from nonliving things?

She flipped the card over and took another drink.

Cathy closed her eyes and counted off on her fingers. There's six, she said. Composed of one or more cells.

Check, Bev said.

They metabolize. They can grow. They can respond to external stimuli.

Bev nodded. Check, check, check.

They can—Cathy hesitated. They can—

Adapt to their surroundings, Bev said.

Cathy's eyes popped open, and when she turned, Bev saw a real flash there, an unfamiliar anger. Don't tell me, Cathy said, and Bev thought of the bears in Asheville. She'd read something about them, but now she couldn't remember what you were supposed to do when a bear attacked. Did you play dead, or did you fight for your life?

She stared at Cathy, a woman she sometimes called her partner. Other times, they called each other friends or even roommates depending on who they were talking to. Cathy's eyes were closed again, and she'd started back at the beginning of the list, and now she was stuck. Now she needed help. All right, Cathy said. She was giving up. What's the last one?

Bev looked down at the card. She read, They can reproduce.

Cathy's hands were fists, and she beat them against her head. Then she actually slapped herself, hard across the face. I knew that, she said. I knew that all along.

Bev reached out, but before she could touch Cathy, before she could say anything, Cathy was picking up all the cards and jamming them into her pockets. There were so many compartments and loops and zippers in those pants, Bev had joked about Cathy carrying bullets and grenades. Like, she said, you're going into combat.

Cathy slid off the stool. I gotta take a leak, she said.

Where are you going? Bev said, even though Cathy had just told her. Everything moved so quickly, and Bev's mind was sluggish. She was still thinking about explosions and bears, the way things sounded so distant when you were underwater. She shook her head, willing what was inside to catch up with all that was happening. Hey, she said, I'll go too.

But Cathy was already gone, already behind the filigreed door that led down into the restaurant. Bev took her drink and slid off the barstool. The glass was cold in her hand, and she felt a deep chill in her chest. In her mind was a song without words. She walked to the edge of the roof.

Reproduce. Respond to stimuli. Adapt to surroundings. Bev remembered studying something like that when she was in school. Surely she had. Sometimes Bev was as forgetful and confused as some of the residents at Twilight, and there were times when she wondered if everyone around her wasn't just saying whatever wouldn't cause trouble, whatever wouldn't wake her up.

That weekend, it was supposed to be sunny in Asheville. Here, though, the sky was gray, and the wind still blew, and with it came a few drops of very cold rain. Soon it would be winter.

Cathy had gone to the bathroom. Of course she had. But she must have also forgotten something in the car because there she was on the street below. Bev could see the top of her head, the white shine of her scalp beneath the short hair. Cathy would make a good paramedic. Once, she'd found a baby squirrel under a tree in the backyard. Bev was certain the squirrel wouldn't make it, but Cathy had nursed the little thing with a bottle until it was ready to live on its own. Everywhere Cathy looked, she saw something worth saving.

There was a time when Bev had felt that way, too.

She hadn't told Cathy about what happened with Mozelle. She hadn't told Cathy about a lot of things. Maybe now was the time. If she told it right, she might even make Cathy laugh.

Bev wanted to call out to Cathy. It would have been strange for them to see one another from such an angle. Bev meant to wave or blow a kiss or stick her thumbs in her ears and wiggle her fingers. She meant to do something, but her voice must have been lost in the cars that passed, in the mounting wind, and as Bev watched, she saw Cathy leaning up against the car. She saw her pull out the cards. She saw her reading the words, memorizing the terms.

Bev stumbled back. She was losing her balance. She was trying to say, I've got to tell you something funny. She was trying to say, Slow down. Easy.

WHERE WE GO

It was June, and Lonnie and Moto were walking the streets. They'd done it the past couple of summers. Propelled by boredom and curiosity and blinding teenage desire, Lonnie and Moto, long tired of their own dumb yards and their own stupid rooms, hit the busted sidewalks just to go some place, any place, but this year something was different.

This year, they were fifteen. Lonnie's shorts were shorter, tighter. Moto hadn't grown much, but now she had a dog, a lanky husky pup ill-suited for the swampy climate of Black Creek, South Carolina. These things weren't the same as they were, but they also didn't make any real difference. The real difference was something else, something that Moto couldn't quite name but was just as tangible as Lonnie's long legs or the panting dog or the rain that didn't fall but hung in the air and made a haze of everything. The real difference moved the hair on the back of Moto's neck. It curled around and tightened against her throat. At night, when she was alone with the pup, she could hardly stand the weight of this new and uncertain fear.

She's so stupid, Lonnie said about her mother. She walked a few steps ahead, and Moto saw the pink flash of her bare feet, the yellow polish on her toes. Lonnie said she didn't need shoes and rolled her eyes when Moto said something about rocks and nails. Don't be a baby, Lonnie said.

Moto watched the feet, the ankles and the more delicate bones, the cords that held everything together.

You're lucky, Lonnie said. She didn't finish the thought. She didn't have to.

Shut up, Moto said.

Lonnie shot her a look. You know what I mean.

Moto was going to say something, but she coughed and swallowed instead. She didn't let other people say things like that, but Lonnie didn't have a dad, and there were other factors that added up to Lonnie being able to talk to Moto like other people couldn't. They'd been friends since the fifth grade. Sometimes she and Moto talked to each other without even speaking at all.

If I were you, Lonnie said, I'd do whatever I wanted.

The pup stopped to sniff the bottom of a rusting mailbox. Moto pulled on his leash. For a second, he tried digging in, setting his stance for the long sniff. But when Moto said, Come on, the pup looked at her. Then the muscles in his hips relaxed, and he did. He came on.

Lonnie was talking about some concert she wanted to go to. Moto didn't know the band, but she pretended. I've heard of them, she said. I think I have.

Yeah. So my mom says she won't take me because I didn't do the dishes or some shit. I don't know.

Moto wrapped the leash around her wrist, one loop and then another.

So, Lonnie said.

Maybe you could wash the dishes. Maybe then she'd let you go.

Lonnie looked back over her shoulder. She was glaring. You always take the other person's side.

Do not.

Do, Lonnie mocked.

Somebody had thrown out a bottle. It was shattered there on the sidewalk, and Moto saw it glittering up ahead. She was about to say something. She was about to give some kind of warning, but Lonnie just walked right through. She never stopped talking, and it was hard to say if she saw the glass and stepped in all the right places or if she just got lucky, but there was Lonnie on the other side and no worse for it.

Moto pulled the pup, guiding him out and around the sharpest pieces. The slivers glittered in the sun, and it was hard to believe it was never anything more than a beer bottle.

They were at the corner of Quinby now and turning down the sidewalk that lined Ferry Road. It was an old street lined with antebellum mansions and oak trees hung with Spanish moss. A few of the houses were in good condition, one kept up by an orthopedic surgeon with a casual interest in real estate. Another by a retired judge turned eccentric. But these nicer homes were closer to the courthouse, and Lonnie and Moto were headed in the other direction.

Down this part of the street, the houses were just as big—some as many as four stories with built-on rooms and attics and wide front porches. But these houses hadn't been painted in years, decades even. The boards were rotted. Sections of roofs were draped in frayed blue tarps. Porch columns leaned and threatened to give way.

As many as six or seven cars crowded around the nearly condemned houses, many of which had been divided into apartments, and in one of these houses, in one of these makeshift apartments, lived a boy with a blue Mohawk that Lonnie was trying, she said, to hook. She pulled up her shorts, rolled down the waistband. Her back went stiff, as if something there hurt when she stepped a certain way.

Mohawk was the bass guitarist in the band that was playing the concert that Lonnie couldn't go to because she didn't wash the dishes, and Moto shouldn't have felt too bad because hardly anyone had ever heard of them, but, Lonnie said, one day, everybody would be singing their songs. He'll be famous, Lonnie said, and the way she said it, being famous seemed like the best thing anyone could be.

Mohawk hadn't lived in the house long. Lonnie had seen him for the first time one day last week. She'd been out walking the streets alone because what else was there? Moto was busy, something with her grandmother.

Lonnie had seen him there on the end of the porch. She told Moto that he was sitting on the rail, plucking a guitar, not a bass. His ultimate goal, Lonnie said, was to be the lead. Lonnie could hear him humming. It sounded a lot like this one song by another band Moto didn't know, but it was probably something else, something really original, Lonnie said.

So Mohawk was playing this guitar, and when he looked up and saw Lonnie, he stopped. She pretended not to see him at first, of course, because that's what you do, but when he waved, she waved back. And then he said hey, and then she said hey, and that's when he told her about the band and the concert, which was this Saturday.

That's it? Moto said when Lonnie finished the telling.

What do you mean that's it? Lonnie said. She made a face that said Moto couldn't be dumber. She seemed almost angry. That is everything.

Now Lonnie was focusing. She threw out her hips and pointed her chin up in the air. In the sun, the pimples across her forehead were an even deeper shade of red. A dry rash crept up from her tank top and spread across her wide bony shoulders. Lonnie was thin, and her legs were long, but she was not a pretty girl, and there was something about her that made the cheerleaders and the beauty queens turn up their noses, as if, about Lonnie, there was a certain and repelling odor. They acted the same way around Moto, but Moto didn't much care about the girls and their clothes and their lip gloss and their boyfriends. Lonnie still cared, though. Lonnie cared a lot.

It was one of these houses, Moto couldn't remember which one exactly, where there used to live an old woman and her brother. Some people said they were witches, but who did those same folks run to, Moto's grandmother said, when they got into trouble? When come Saturday night, they lost their minds and laid down with dogs, Mama Powell said. They didn't wake up praying. That's for sure. They woke up Sunday, and there they were with them dogs and a nest of fleas, or there they were on their way to having some pup, and then those same folks who liked to say witch-this and witch-that were hotfooting it down to Old Man and Sister. That's what Mama Powell said.

Moto tried to tell Lonnie this story once, but she started at the wrong place—when the woman was a teacher before anybody knew she was a witch—and Lonnie said, Nobody cares about all that old stuff.

Ahead, Moto saw Lonnie's shoulders slump. Her butt went flat, and her walk went back to the familiar heavy drag. Mohawk was nowhere to be found.

The pup pulled. He wasn't full-grown, but he wasn't little anymore either, and his muscles were tight ropes. A few houses down, there was a woman who kept a flock of geese. The pup scented the air, let loose a thin whimper.

Want to make the block? Moto said, but Lonnie was already turning around.

Let's just go, she said. She doubled back on Moto, passed her. This is stupid.

Lonnie walked on, and Moto stood there a minute between her friend and the pup. She could have kept going on her own. She didn't have to stay with Lonnie, but something pulled her back. It was the thing she couldn't name, the difference that made her feel like she might scream as she saw Lonnie getting further and further away. Moto had the sense that both of them were walking along a steep edge even though there was the sidewalk and there was the street, same as it had always been.

She jerked the leash, harder than she meant to, and the pup, caught off guard, lurched and scrambled on long legs to catch himself. Come on, Moto said, as if either of them had a choice.

≈

We could, Moto said, go to the park.

The park was not the kind of park with a slide and swings and a merry-go-round. It was a nature park, swampland mostly that was all around Black Creek. Lonnie always said it was so ugly.

Maybe we'll see a snake, Moto said.

Lonnie didn't answer. She just kept moving.

Moto tried again. We go to the cemetery.

I don't believe in that junk, Lonnie said. I'm over it.

To hear Lonnie talk, a person would think years had passed, but it was just that spring they'd hauled a box of candles and a blanket up to the cemetery. They'd sat on one of the graves and, holding each other's hands, they'd tried to perform a séance like something Moto had seen on TV. Nothing had happened, but maybe there were things they couldn't sense, things they couldn't measure. They didn't have all the right equipment. If we just had a thermal imager, Moto had said, which was something else she'd seen on TV. She remembered the heat of Lonnie's hands in her own, the flinch of Lonnie's thumb.

Now Moto wasn't sure what she believed. Were there really such things as witches, or was it just a story that, like a lot of stories, her grandmother had made up to scare her? Once, Moto thought she'd seen her mother, a kind of quick-moving shadow in the corner. She slept in her mother's old room, so it made sense, but then again, Moto's mother wasn't dead. She was just gone.

I hate this place, Lonnie said.

They were making the corner again and now stepping over the same broken glass. Only this time, Lonnie wasn't so lucky. This time, she stepped just right or, really, just wrong, and when Moto heard the yelp, she already knew what had happened.

Moto ran to catch up. The pup, excited by the quickness of Moto's pace, strained. He was sniffing the air, the blood—a thick dark line that traced its way from the ball of Lonnie's foot where a shard of thick green glass was stuck deep.

Lonnie's face twisted in pain. She swiveled her body and sat down in the grass. She held her foot in the air, and a heavy drop of blood fell and splattered against the hot cement.

Moto felt a lurching in her chest. The hand that held the leash was a fist, and she wanted to hit Lonnie with it. I told you, she said.

Lonnie narrowed her eyes. Air came out through her teeth.

Moto passed the leash to her other hand. She uncurled her fingers and reached out. Even before she'd touched the foot, Lonnie howled.

I'm gonna pull it out, Moto said. We have to.

Lonnie started screaming even more then. She tried to jerk away—Let me go! she yelled—but Moto held on. Be still, Moto said. She had to shout to be heard, and they were this way—like much younger children, screaming at each other and wrestling there on the side of the road—when the man came up behind them.

Here, he said, let me.

His voice wasn't deep, but all the same, there was something authoritative about it. Or maybe it was his impressive height or the baldness or the way he seemed to simply appear when they needed someone the most. Whatever it was, both girls responded with a kind of surprised and obedient silence, and when he stepped between them, Moto sort of staggered backward with a feeling that only later, she would recognize as relief. She reached down for the pup, and although he had not barked or even growled, Moto was surprised to find that the hair on the back of his neck was stiff.

I'm David, he said

Like in the Bible, Lonnie said

David looked at her. Like my uncle.

David squatted down. He looked at Lonnie's foot, but he didn't touch it. Yellow is nice, he said. Yellow's my favorite color.

It's green, Moto went to say, thinking he meant the glass, but then she remembered the polish on Lonnie's toes. It was a nasty shade like what the sky turned just before a storm.

Yellow like yell out, David said. That's where the word comes from.

Lonnie blinked. Mellow yellow, she said. That's all I know. She laughed and sniffed all at once.

Moto hadn't noticed until now, but at some point, Lonnie must have been crying.

David was smiling. Lost your shoes?

Lonnie's cheeks were wet. Her bottom lip was puffy. I forgot 'em, she said.

You didn't forget, Moto said, but nobody seemed to hear.

Well, David said, bet you remember from now on. Sometimes we gotta learn the hard way.

He told them he had some tweezers and peroxide. Right over there, he said, and tipped his chin toward the red brick house. It had a little front porch with an arched doorway, like something out of a fairy tale if you didn't look too close.

We're okay, Moto said. She adjusted her grip on the pup's collar. She could take the glass out herself. She knew she could. Thanks anyway.

David turned toward her. He was a big man, but his eyes were small, and they seemed to dull when he turned them on Moto. Where'd you get the wolf? he asked.

Moto looked down at the pup. He's not a wolf.

I know a wolf when I see one.

Lonnie moaned, and it was a sound like a cat made. It was hard to tell what it meant. She can't walk like this, David said.

She can hop, Moto said.

Will it hurt? Lonnie asked, and David said not for long. He bent down and picked her up, and she might have been nothing at all for what little pause her body caused him.

Wait, Moto said as David carried Lonnie across the street.

Moto was about to say more, but over David's shoulder, Lonnie was making a clear and distinct face. She was talking without talking. David was making his way up the stairs now. The closer Moto got, the more teeth Lonnie showed.

At the door, he stopped and turned. Sorry, he said and glanced at the pup, allergies.

Moto looked down. The pup's mouth was open. His long pink tongue dripped. I'll tie him up, Moto said.

No! Lonnie said. She yelled it, but when David looked down at her, she added, in a changed voice, He'll run away.

The pup had broken loose before, twice since Moto had gotten him—once to chase a squirrel, the other time to chase a car.

I'll take him home then. I'll put him in the house.

This won't be a minute, David said, and Lonnie said, Yeah, Moto. Just a minute, all right?

Lonnie and David were inside the house now, and there was a certain smell that came from the paneled darkness, and it wasn't terrible exactly, but even still, Moto didn't like it, and the words seemed to burst out of her like the swift swing of a fist that's bound to miss: We don't know you!

David had eased Lonnie down on her one good foot. Lonnie stood there, with her knee bent like some delicate bird, and David stared at Moto, studied her. He was sorry again, this time for shutting the door. Air conditioning, he explained. He explained everything, and even though Moto was thinking the worst—kidnappers and abusers and molesters—it was true that those sorts of things didn't really happen in Black Creek, and David looked pretty much like a regular guy. David was big, but he didn't leer or drool like the videos of perverts they showed in school. When Moto looked at him, she really didn't see much of an expression at all, and once he'd shut the door, she wasn't sure she could even describe him if someone had asked. Squinty eyes, she might say. Bald. He could have been her math teacher. Or the principal. Or the mailman.

For a minute, Moto stared at her own reflection in the door's glass pane. She was trying to figure out what to do. She might have barged in after them. If the door was locked, she could have broken the window and turned the knob from the inside. The important part was to wrap your hand in a T-shirt. She'd seen that in a movie and was pretty sure she could do it. She had a cell phone in her pocket. She could dial 9-1-1 and say her friend had been abducted, but had she?

Over David's shoulder, Lonnie had given Moto a hard look, and the message was clear. Tell him we love him, Lonnie had said that day at the cemetery. No matter what Lonnie said now, Moto knew there was a minute when she wanted to believe. Tell him we loved him. That might work.

In the glass, Moto's face was round. Her hair was in a ponytail. She might have been twelve, eleven even.

She spun around, yanking hard on the leash. She fell into one of the chairs on the porch. There was an ashtray full of butts. Moto took one of the filters, sniffed it, and threw it back on the pile. Sometimes she thought Lonnie was right. Sometimes she hated this place, too.

Moto waited, listening but hearing nothing except the birds in the trees. Across the street, a woman was working in her yard. She had a shovel, and she nearly stood on the end of the blade to cut into the dirt. She bent and hefted, and in her thin pale arms, the shovel seemed very heavy, but the woman just kept working. Her face was a shadow under a hat. Her overalls hung loose. Moto imagined the woman was digging a grave. Then she imagined that *she* was that woman, that *she* was the one holding the shovel.

The pup was thirsty. He licked at her fingers, and Moto patted him on the head. She told him it was okay, even though she didn't think it was, and right then, she wasn't sure it ever would be again.

≈

Moto's grandmother was dying and had been for some time now. Mama Powell had known it from the beginning, when she first started feeling the pains in her belly. She reminded Moto of all the things she'd done for her, namely taking her in when no one else would. Moto would be in the wind if it weren't for her. She made Moto promise, made her swear that she wouldn't take her to some hospital or over to Twilight, where she'd get filled up with needles and tubes and medicine that would only make her sicker. She wanted to die at home, in her own bed, quietly and with some peace. Swear to me, Makeisha, she said because this was the girl's real name and not something some other fool girl—Lonnie—had made up. Swear to me on your mother.

And Moto did swear, though at the time, she couldn't know all that her promise would mean.

Mama Powell, true to her intuition, had gotten sicker and sicker, and when she could no longer get out of bed, Moto half-expected the rush of a crowd. A doctor. A preacher. Other old ladies. But her grandmother was a private woman who, after a certain preacher left, quit going to church though Moto believed the truth was that her grandmother didn't much feel like going anymore. No one knew she was ill, and sometimes Moto wondered if anyone even knew they existed. Mostly at night when the street lights were the shade of the sun caught behind a thunderhead and beyond their odd glow, the darkness was cast even deeper, it seemed to Moto like she and her grandmother were the last people in the world.

And now Mama Powell hardly seemed like a person at all. She didn't talk anymore or in any way fend for herself. Moto fed her spoonfuls of chicken broth and changed her diapers and did her best, with a bucket of warm soapy water, to give her grandmother a bath.

This had been terrible at first, the baths somehow even more embarrassing than the diapers, but now, Moto was used to it. Though her grandmother's skin was old and loose and miraculously wrinkled, it was, to Moto, no different than a child's, and she cleansed it out of love and necessity and ritual. Gently, she ran the rag across her grandmother's chest and the soft belly where, she sometimes remembered, her own mother had once been.

It's amazing, Lonnie said, to be that close to a person.

It was Friday, the day after Lonnie had cut her foot, and in that time, she'd told Moto—multiple times and in great detail—all of what had happened between her and David inside the red brick house. It had started in the bathroom where, true to his word, David had taken out the piece of glass. He hadn't had peroxide after all but only a bottle of alcohol, which had burned. When Lonnie said so, said that she was hurting worse than she'd ever hurt before, he'd blown on her heel. Then he'd kissed her foot—Imagine, Lonnie said—and then her leg and then other parts of her, and then he'd carried her to the bedroom, to the water bed. It was, she said, everything she thought it would be. I get it now, she said. I get all of it.

Moto wanted to ask what there was to get, but she didn't.

They were at the cemetery, not because they were trying to talk to ghosts—Lonnie didn't do that stuff anymore— but because the cemetery was their meeting place. Lonnie sat on a thick granite tombstone with her foot propped on the head of an angel.

Moto listened to the story until it was finished. Her breath came quick. There was a soreness at the back of her throat, but her face must not have registered the thrill or the admiration or whatever it was that Lonnie was after.

Lonnie scraped at a pimple on her forehead in the way that she always did when she was irritated. In the past, she might have yelled at Moto. And now, she opened her mouth, but she seemed to catch herself. She smiled instead and said that Moto just didn't get it. She wasn't mature enough. One day, Lonnie said, Moto would understand. One day, Moto would understand everything.

Moto was pacing around a certain plot she favored. The pup was laying in the shade. His tongue lolled, and though he sometimes looked at Moto, his tail did not move, and she had the sense he was not seeing her at all.

That wolf, Lonnie said. You got a name for it yet?

There wasn't any thought in what Moto did next. She just moved, lunged at Lonnie and grabbed her by the front of the shirt. He ain't no wolf, she said.

Their faces were close together, and Moto could feel Lonnie's breath on her face, and Lonnie was mad, but Moto was madder.

Let me go, Lonnie said, and when Moto still held her, she said it again. Let me go, I said!

Finally, Moto turned loose, and Lonnie staggered back. She rolled her shoulders, adjusted the neck of her shirt. She squinted at Moto.

I said we shouldn't come here anymore. It's stupid.

Moto looked around at the stones. She knew the names and even some of the dates by heart.

But this is where we go. This is what we do.

Lonnie shrugged.

And now, Saturday, Lonnie was gone. Her mother had taken her to Mohawk's concert after all. Moto couldn't go, not because she wasn't allowed but because she had to take care of her grandmother. Lonnie said she'd just go by herself then, but Moto wasn't so sure. Moto thought maybe Lonnie had asked some other girl.

Moto finished with her grandmother's bath. She set the bucket of soapy water down on the rag rug. She took the soft thin towel and dried the places that were still wet. Then she squeezed out some lotion and warmed it between her hands before rubbing it into her grandmother's elbows, her knees, her ankles.

The old woman barely blinked. There was something in her eyes that reminded Moto of an animal, a bear she'd seen on a field trip to the zoo. Even though the bear turned in a circle and kicked a soccer ball, and played dead, he looked like, at any moment, he might bite.

There was one person who knew about her grand-mother's condition, and that was Moto's father. Jerry dropped by at times that were never predictable. Some-times, he came twice a month, but a year might pass when Moto didn't see him at all. He and Mama Powell had never gotten along. The old woman didn't think Jerry was good enough for her daughter, Moto's mother, and there was a time, early on, when she was probably right. Occasionally, Jerry brought money when he came, but most of the time, he asked for it.

Moto signed her grandmother's social security checks and cashed them at the gas station down by the bridge, and out of this, she'd give her father ten dollars, sometimes five if she felt it was all she could spare. You got a heart of gold, girl, Jerry told her once, but Moto knew this wasn't true.

Her grandmother wore a thin cross around her neck, and it shone and caught the light even in the dark bedroom. It was gold, and no matter how long Moto stared at it, it was nothing like what she felt. Whatever was in Moto's chest was sharp and cold, and lately it seemed to grow and turn upon itself in ways that made Moto feel like something ter-rible was happening.

Things change, Lonnie had said. It seemed like the worst part of the world, and yet there were times when it was all Moto wanted, for everything to be different than what it was.

She looked down at her grandmother, this naked, wast-ed body that did not speak, that only stared without seeing. It could be over. Fast and easy. It was, like breaking into houses, a trick she'd learned from the movies. Moto's hands moved for the pillow. Or she might have done it with the necklace, turning it, tightening it until it was over. No, it could not have been gold in Moto's heart, but what it was would remain there, a twisted scrap, because from outside, from that impenetrable night, came a yelp and a snap.

The sound stopped Moto where she was and then drew her to the porch where she'd tied the pup and where now, from the cheap metal rail, hung only a section of rope. Moto looked out into that darkness. During the day, Black Creek was so humid, you'd swear you were walking through a cloud, but some nights, the air seemed to thin, and like a kind of vacuum, it could take your breath away. In the streetlight, the moths and the June bugs floated and spun like motes, nearly weightless.

There was no sign of the dog, there or beyond, but Moto went out anyway. She glanced back, but from here, she couldn't see her grandmother. She stepped outside and pulled the door closed behind her.

≈

She went out into that black night. The other times the pup had broken loose, he hadn't gone far—just to the stop sign or to the bottom of an ancient oak tree where in the branches a tensed squirrel crouched in a last posture of defense. But now, the dog was nowhere Moto could see, and she could barely see at all.

Still, as if playing by the rules of some unusual gravity, she half-walked and half-ran the streets alone, whistling in that way that was meant to draw things. It must have been nearly midnight. Most of the houses were dark, but in one, lit from within, the curtains moved and a face appeared. A face appeared but no door opened.

Moto searched the darkness for some glimmer, some reflection. The pup had been a present from her father. He'd got it up in Minnesota on one of what he called his routes. He told her that it was a purebred husky, papered he'd said, but he'd lost all that somewhere between there and here, and now the pup's eyes weren't as blue as they had been, and he'd thinned out considerably. He didn't look like the pictures of huskies Moto had seen. She'd checked some books out from the library. She was afraid he really might be something else, something wild.

And now that she loved him, now that she'd lost him, she didn't know what to do. Those streets that she'd walked with Lonnie a thousand times had turned to paths cut in the thickets of some other planet. She felt that clinch in her throat. The air in her chest came even faster, shorter.

She very nearly ran down Quinby and then Ferry Road, by the very house where the witches had lived. People thought the woman might have put a curse on Black Creek, but Mama Powell said that was dumb stuff. The whole world was cursed and that had happened nearly two thousand years ago, and the best anybody could do was try to find some peace.

Moto wasn't sure what peace really was, but maybe it had something to do with everything Moto was supposed to understand, the *it* Lonnie said she would get one day.

Moto was never more alone than in that moment, and yet, she sensed she was being watched. If only she could find the pup. If only Lonnie was there, if only someone was.

Glass broke beneath her shoes. She had made the turn and was back on Quinby. There ahead was the house where she'd seen the woman in the yard, the woman digging. And there across the street was the red brick where she'd sat with the pup.

She whistled again, as if the dog might have come back to this familiar place, but it was Moto who was being drawn. It was Moto who moved by instinct.

She crossed the road. She moved from one side to the other, and she did not look both ways or even any way. She was climbing those steps and knocking on the door, and when David appeared she said, I want you to do to me what you did to Lonnie.

David did not turn on the porch light, and so in that darkness, Moto could not see his face. She didn't need to.

What I did, he said.

I told you, she said. I want you to do it to me, too.

Maybe a minute passed. Maybe it was only a few seconds. But eventually, David stepped back and Moto stepped in.

Lonnie had said that one day Moto would understand, and this was what Moto wanted more than anything. She wanted to stop imagining what things could be. She wanted to make sense of the way things were. She wanted to be grown because grown people didn't seem to hurt as much. They didn't seem to feel a whole lot of anything, and maybe this was it. Maybe this was peace.

David made almost no noise on top of her. It happened fast and indistinctly, and it didn't matter that none of Lonnie's details were right—that it wasn't a waterbed, that David didn't have a blue fish in a jar or a mirror on the ceiling. All of this was just a part of a story and nothing that made a difference, not even the toy planes which hung suspended over the bed.

There was a time when Moto thought this moment would make her more like Lonnie, more like all the other people in the world, but lying there in the bed and staring up at the ceiling, she thought only of her grandmother. Pain and then a welcome numbness spread throughout her body. She thought it came from outside, from some distance, that series of yips and the long lowering howl. Moto's eyes were open, and like an animal's, caught the light and she saw then that even when it came fast—as sudden as a pillow over the face or a gold chain pulled taut—a person didn't go out of this world all at once. The leaving started early and it happened in pieces that were as mean and jagged and beautiful as broken glass, and once some things were gone, it didn't matter if you knew what had been lost. There was still no way to call it back.

ABOUT THOSE PLANES

They're almost there.

Sweat beads above Lynn's lip, mottling the heavy powder she's daubed. Under her hair, too, at the back of her neck and around her ears—this damp heat, and also, in her mouth, the grit and bile of salt that has settled and persisted in the eight—no, seven—months since she moved with Ed to Myrtle Beach. The ocean won't turn loose of Lynn even when they're driving away from it. Oh God. Jesus and Joseph. She grabs at the vents, diamonds casting giddy lights. We're almost there, she says, more to herself than to Ed because really, when you get right down to it, Ed isn't all that pleasant to talk to. Lynn quit trying almost as soon as she started. We're almost there.

What'd you mean? Ed says and calls her silly. Silly old goose. We *are* there. Don't you see we're here?

Lynn turns her head, and when she does, it's as if the edges of the world blur and run like those watercolor beach scenes she and every other old lady and some old men try to paint. Idiots in white linen. Thin skin burning. At the beach because where else? That's how Ed put it. Everything is so easy for him. The beach is where the old people go, and so they went, and it is like so much else Lynn had done in that she did it without question. That is to say, all the questions came too late.

There are houses and trees and mailboxes, and if Lynn focuses the center of her vision, she can see, she can certainly *read* the sign that says Quinby Place, but nothing looks the same. Nothing looks right, and she turns to tell Ed because even though he's nothing to talk to, Ed is like Myrtle Beach in that, for Lynn, there doesn't seem to be an alternative, but when Lynn opens her mouth, it's Ed's voice—gravel and gruff—saying, There, see.

He's pulling over, the ridiculous white and chrome hulk of an SUV, so oversized even Ed calls it The Rig. Ed's vision isn't what it used to be, and he scrapes the curb with a tire. There's a sharp grinding sound like something heavy about to give way, and Lynn blinks and sees her very own porch, the red brick arches that made her say, the first time she saw it, Hansel and Gretel.

It's little wonder, though, that Lynn didn't know it at first—the yard all gone to weeds and grown up and all her wicker porch furniture gone not with her and Ed to Myrtle Beach but to the Salvation Army. And the paint around the windows flaking, and even though that one shutter had always hung crooked, it is, Lynn notes, more crooked now. There is about the whole place a sense of sag—longer than seven months worth—that does more than irritate Lynn. The disrepair, the passing of time and neglect that's caused it, scares Lynn nearly to the point of phobia. This is a fear she knows well, a tremor at the edges, which is how Lynn sees the world. Her neck, her arms, but more than her body—Lynn is smart enough to know she can't put any stock into that anymore—what's inside, everything spinning in an unsteady wobble, and David at the center of it. David coming out of the house, and he is pale, and he is swollen, and he is nothing like what Lynn ever wanted him to be, but here he is, opening the door. Here he is still calling her Mama.

There had never been much touching when David was little. Lynn herself had been raised the same way, as if at a distance, but now David embraces her. They say affection is important. They say humans and other animals don't develop properly without it. David's arms are around her, and she pats his shoulders. She can smell him as strongly as when he was a teenager, and he is soft. He yields in ways a man shouldn't.

Ed, for all his faults and his failing eyes, is still, at seventy-six, a hard man. Even his belly, which is a low and small paunch, is so firm that Lynn's finger bounces back when she teases him, pokes him there. When she's in a better way than she is now.

Ed pops the great hatch of the monstrous SUV and hollers for David to come help with the bags, and in the backseat, on the hook, the tuxes and Lynn's sailor dress.

Go help, Lynn says and waves David away so that she can begin the process of dismounting what amounts, in her mind, to a military tank. It's like we're going to war, she said, the first time Ed took her out in it, and she meant to be funny, but what she said wasn't funny at all.

In the little carport beside the house, she sees the blue Buick she drove for thirty years, the car that David still drives. A few weeks ago, David had to get some work done on it—new belts, a general fluid flushing. A long mysterious process that would cost a couple of thousand dollars, and Lynn said, Don't do it. You ought to get something else, something sporty.

And David said he'd think about it, but in the end, he'd had the work done, said he liked that car, didn't say he didn't want a new one, that he couldn't bear that change or any other, but Lynn knew it to be true all the same as she signed her name to the check and mailed it to him. This—the going-along with whatever David wanted and calling it support, calling it love—was so much easier than the physical contact all the experts said was so important or so Lynn read in all the right books as she thought about David and about her own childhood and what was missing.

The weather, the roads, the traffic, which there was none of. Soon, Ed will have exhausted all his topics of conversation. He's closed the hatch, and he's pulling the suitcase behind him just like he pulls his golf clubs, like he's waiting for somebody else to take over. And David is carrying Lynn's overnight case and holding the garment bags, the dress and the two tuxedos, out away from him like a person will hold anything he doesn't trust.

Don't drag, Lynn says, and David lifts his arm up higher.

Up the sidewalk and the stairs and on the porch, and Lynn saying, What happened to all my roses? And Lynn saying, Even weeds ought to be mowed. And Lynn seeing the tray of butts and saying, I thought you quit. And Lynn hearing herself say all this, Lynn hearing herself rattle because a part of her, because most of her, is somewhere else, higher than all this. Most of her is quiet and watching these things unfold. Most of her wonders what it is she says and why she even bothers.

A darkness in the house. An absence of light, but also something else, shadows magnified by the very brightness of the day, and it's strange to be back in the place one used to live. Strange to see, as Lynn does, some of her old furniture because, despite Ed's best efforts, they hadn't gotten rid of everything she owned—the junk, Ed called it. They had been in the process of going through the junk when Lynn told David, when she couldn't put it off any longer. She told him that she and Ed were married and moving to Myrtle Beach, and David said, Don't, and Lynn said, It's too late, and David said, Then I'm moving back.

He'd been married, too—David had. For a short time, and Lynn knew it was doomed from the start even though she'd been the one to shoo David out of the house. She'd been the one to tell him he needed to live his own life, take some classes, get a job, something. He'd tried, he said. He'd done his best, but marriage, for David, was just another thing adults were supposed to do, no different than getting a driver's license or voting.

David isn't stupid. In fact, he's very smart about, for example, taking things apart and putting them together again. But he doesn't feel like other people. For David, it's all or nothing, and for anyone other than Lynn—his teachers, his wife—David's emotions, his attitudes are difficult to predict. But Lynn understands that it doesn't matter if David is thirty-six or sixty-three because, in this way, in the manner he reacts to the world, he will always be fifteen. There isn't much else that Lynn knows with such certainty.

There on the table is another one of David's airplanes, the models he assembles by what seems like the thousands. And Ed says as he passes through to the bedroom, See you got a new toy, and Lynn wants to slap him across the face because he's cruel and nobody to talk to, and nothing is as simple as all that. She wants to slap David, too, for the airplane, for letting her roses go, for lots of things. For a minute there, she'd felt some better, but now she feels worse, and she, the old goose, stumbles around in the dark house until she remembers, yes, down the hall and to the right. Close the door. Turn the lock. See the face in the

mirror—pale and lined and sometimes only vaguely familiar. See a life as it was and as it is now and as it will be, eventually, no longer at all. Lynn isn't surprised by the sickness,
by the waves that come up from her toes.

What is strange, Lynn thinks, is how a person can keep
from doubling over. What is a miracle is that some days we
manage to hold straight and keep our feet flat on the ground.

≈

Lynn washes her face. Then she changes her mind and
turns on the tub faucet as hot as hot will go. The tub isn't
clean like she kept it, but there is a bottle of Mr. Bubble,
which Lynn opens and pours under the running water until
the foam begins to stack.

What're you doing? *Knock, knock,* and it's Ed saying it's
the middle of the afternoon, saying we just got here, saying,
A bath? Now? Lynn. He jerks the doorknob.

Lynn eyes the swiveling brass, the lock that catches, and
for a minute, she tricks herself into believing that on the
other side of the door is a criminal. On the other side of the
door is a person with only bad intentions. The knob shakes
one way and then the other, and within Lynn, there is that
turning of fear, a genuine surge of dread and panic. Stop
it, she yells, and she tells herself she has to be heard over
the water, but underneath the fear, there's an anger, a frustration that is every bit as solid as the faucet she grips and
turns. Just stop already, she screams. Can't you hear I'm in
the tub? I'm in the tub, Ed!

She's on the *edge* of the tub, still in her clothes, crouched
and listening, and on the other side of the door, the thug,
the creep, the enemy says, All right, all right, and something

else Lynn doesn't hear because, finally, he's gone. Finally, he's left her.

He'll hate her for this, for leaving him alone with David no sooner than they got here, he'll say. You know how me and him get on, and what he means is not at all. What he means is David doesn't get on with anyone.

Lynn pushes herself up from the side of the tub. She undresses and eases over the side. She's started hanging onto things. Her hands at the end of the day are a grimy mess. She feels herself clinging. Stair rails and door knobs and when there is nothing else, at the very walls around her. She's had some trouble with her hip, and at her age, she knows, there is always the danger of falling. Several women from the watercolor group have gone down just in the past few months. Broken ankle. Broken leg. Broken wrist from the hand that tried in vain, too late to catch the body's weight. And then the hospital and the rehab. And then the nursing home. The very earth on which they stood pitched and rolled so that they were always fighting against it, and Lynn would have preferred to retire to any place besides the ocean, any place that seemed steadier.

But even now she's pulled toward the water. Mr. Bubble smells like bubblegum, the kind she chewed as a girl— that initial brilliant, if fleeting, sweetness. She leans back and closes her eyes and against such darkness, and sometimes now in the light, certain pictures appear. This time a feather-capped lady and an elephant in dirty sequins and Lynn's own body, fifteen herself and so strong, she might have stepped right up and swung from the trapeze out of the crowd and into the rafters. She had the feeling anyway, when she caught just the right line with her charcoal. Some of her best work, those sketches at the circus. Real promise.

She feels better—more herself, she thinks—as she gets out of the water, towels herself off, and crosses the hall to get dressed. Comfortable clothes, all cotton and elastic, and her hair up and cool, and in the kitchen, Ed and David are eating sandwiches, and there are times when Lynn experiences a disturbing terror, but there are spaces, too, when things smear in such a way as to create an altogether different scene, say not enemies but a father and a son sharing a meal. Say a loving mother pouring up a glass of lemonade. Say her telling them and a part of her believing, I'm so glad we're here. We're going to have a great time.

≈

She met Ed at an oyster bake. It was the sort of event put on by the sort of people who never forget to consider the widows. And this is how they think of Lynn now that she's old, now that enough time has passed that people forget or choose not to remember or just don't care about what really happened. To them, Lynn's no different than old Clarice Powell and the lady, Miriam, from down the street. Lynn doesn't think of herself as a widow, but maybe she is, maybe Gary is dead. He might have been dead for years, and she wouldn't know. No one would think to call.

It dawns on Lynn that maybe somewhere people think Gary is a widower. Maybe they imagine Lynn is dead. And she tries to picture herself, a ghost haunting the other side of the country. Somehow, it feels right. It feels right and good.

The oyster bake was a year ago February, and by that time, David was already divorced but still living in Columbia doing something or other. Computers. Systems. Something. His apartment there, his life there, is to Lynn a kind of haze, a phase she didn't really have time to understand before it was over.

And that time in her own life isn't much clearer. She doesn't remember how it happened between her and Ed, the particulars of it anyway. Only that they met at this oyster bake and then there were some lunches and dinners and sometime in all that she became aware that Ed lived comfortably. There was the golf course and the big house and, of course, the The Rig, and, too, the plans that Ed, like every other well-to-do fogy within a two-hundred-mile radius, had made to retire to Myrtle Beach.

And maybe there was some excitement at first. Some flutter of real happiness, but in the end, it all seemed like something Lynn let happen more than anything Lynn actually desired. Her whole life, up until that moment, was year after year of waiting. Even before Gary left, it seemed she was only biding her time until she became someone different. A famous artist. A better mother. Things she couldn't even name. When Ed came along, she was nearly at the end of it all, and she was worn out, and if nothing else, Ed was a kind of final act, and so she said, Okay. Yes. Myrtle Beach. Or at least she didn't say no.

Bizarre, she would describe a world—this world—in which she found herself getting ready, re-powdering her face and lining her eyes so that she might stand before an audience at the Black Creek Land Trust Ball and introduce this man—her newlywed husband—the oldest living member of the board, who now, in the living room, snored and twitched as he napped, his paunch made paunchier by the hoagie roll and tuna he'd eaten with David.

Absurd the way time moved and didn't, and her gimping down the hall to check on her son, the troubled forever-boy who could not be trusted to rent his own tuxedo, who even now was getting dressed in the very room in which he grew up, the room in which from the ceiling hung what must have been a hundred model airplanes, and all of it starting with just the one, the dime-store Sesna Lynn bought and wrapped and gave as a present from David's father who was—Lynn told the boy—traveling on business.

She shouldn't have done that. She shouldn't have lied to him. They think honesty is best now, people do. The people who write the books Lynn reads even though it's too late to change anything. They think it's always better to tell children the truth even when it hurts. Especially when it does.

It strikes Lynn that all these planes make for a kind of elaborate mobile, and she thinks of David as a baby, the way he would reach for the shapes even as he fell asleep. But when Lynn looks up, all she sees are mistakes, a thousand perfect miniatures of everything she might have done differently.

And now here he is in front of her, dressed in a tuxedo that draws new lines about his person. His shoulders are squarer, his legs made to look longer, and he's showered and shaved, too. You look great, she says and means it. You look just wonderful.

She reaches up for the loose ends of the tie.

All sorts of lies she told. About the airplane. About just what it was they were doing those nights they drove out to Paulie's and sat in the Buick. David held the flashlight while she worked on her drawings, the sketch pad propped against the steering wheel. And she told him all kinds of things about colors and lines and how real artists worked among the people. She told him about the circus and the lady turning flips in the air. Real artists, she said, see things that nobody else does. She taught him about the angle of a nose, the slant of a neck, that true beauty was all a measure of symmetry. It all comes down to balance.

And in the meantime, as she sketched, she studied the faces, and she was pretending to be an artist when all she could be was a wife who'd been left by a sad drunk who didn't know how to be a father. All she could do was search for one thing and then another—the features of a husband, the hollows of cheeks that would be even more pronounced there under the floodlight that marked the joint's entrance. Paulie's had been one of Gary's favorite places, and if he was tempted to come back to Black Creek, he might come here, and it was worth a try, she thought. It was worth something, at least until the bulb in the flashlight began to flicker or until David nodded off, and then it seemed like there was nothing more pointless, nothing that was more of a waste than this. More nights than not, Lynn tore out those sketches and threw them out the window of the Buick. Behind them, in the flush of the taillights, the shapes of Paulie's regulars, the old faithfuls—the warts and lumps, the squints and cleavage and amputations—all of these shapes and lines were captured and, at once, released to the darkness, and in her brighter moments, Lynn wonders what better truth there is to tell a child, what greater testament than this.

She ties the tie, and she knows David doesn't want to go to the Black Creek Land Trust Ball, knows it is, in fact, the very last thing he wants to do. Naturally, he would rather be at the table with his glue and his paintbrush, and these planes of his. There's a real beauty to them, an attention to detail, and some of what Lynn desired—a great proportion of it, really—was for David to be happy like she never could be, and he's put on the suit to please her. He's doing this because she's asked him to, and suddenly, inexplicably, Lynn is afraid again. Lynn begins to shake, and in her ears, there is a kind of roaring which is not unlike the sound of a thousand planes or the rush of the ocean, the horror of what will come next, and then just as quickly, just before it drives Lynn to her knees, things go quiet. Things go absolutely still except for David who is leaning down, David who is asking, What's wrong? What is it?

Nothing, she says and swats at the air as if at a wasp, as if a wasp was all.

≈

Lynn's dress is navy with gold trim, beaded and long-sleeved. It is very ugly, she thinks, and she feels very ugly in it. David tells her otherwise, but David isn't here now. David's back at the house. David will come later, he says, though Lynn wonders if he'll come at all. Or if instead, dressed in the tux, he'll sit down at the table and get working on one of his planes. He loses time, that way, and people, too. He's told her before, It's like being somewhere else.

At the club, Lynn does what she ought—meeting people, pretending to remember having met them before. All of the women are in mother-of-the-bride dresses, but on Lynn, such a dress feels like more of a costume. She trips over her hem, tugs at the neckline as if the thing were fitted to someone else.

Here, Ed is in his element, and Lynn isn't surprised to find herself, for a while, alone at a table cluttered with dishes and silverware and stemmed glasses. She doesn't even mind it really, the way all these people get on with Ed. He can talk to *them*, all right. But at least she has these minutes to herself. Time enough to look for David. Time enough to pretend she is elsewhere—Arizona or Nevada, a figure so slight as to be more of a feeling, a brush on a cheek, little more than a breeze, than a shadow saying, Here I am.

Soon, though, everyone makes their way to the tables, and the piano stops, and someone takes a hold of the microphone. A young man, about David's age, talking about a hometown girl who married a hometown boy, and what does it matter if their love came later rather than sooner in life, and aren't they the lucky ones to live now, as they do, in a condo on the beach where nobody wears a watch, and somewhere in all the gab, in the tangle of congratulatory cliché, Lynn realizes with a start that the man is talking about her.

Then everyone is clapping, and there is a hand at her back, pushing her forward, and she is moving. Yes, she is drifting between the round tables which are like so many islands, and Lynn in her anchors and gold rope is not anything like the wind but is, instead, a heavy ship, some kind of tanker that moves nowhere of its own accord.

Up the stairs. Onto the stage, and hand by hand, the clapping stops. The room then is so very quiet, and everyone is staring at Lynn, the silly goose, who's having a hard time now remembering just exactly what it is she's doing. She smiles at the crowd, and they smile back. A patient group. Not so bad when you get down to it. And someone out there yells, Speech! Then a ripple of laughter, patient but uneasy.

Lynn's hand fumbles at her side, and her thumb catches in the pockets they make in such dresses, pockets meant for tissues because the mother of the bride is always crying, because never is there not some shade of despair, and that's the truth, and her thumb catches the pocket, and she finds the cards on which she wrote the words to introduce the oldest living member of the board who is, oh yes, her husband, and she looks at the cards, and the writing is hers, the lines familiar and yet wholly illegible. What words are these she doesn't know, and she says something in the microphone—what?—and the faces in the crowd smear and run, and Lynn herself isn't a ship after all. She's more like the water, more nothing than anything, and David is there, but they aren't in the building anymore. She isn't on stage, and they aren't in the country club, but they must have been because there they are, still in the tuxedo and the dress, Lynn's skirt fanned across the seat of the Buick.

What a picture we are, Lynn says. This isn't what she means, but David must know. Too late, the question comes: What happened?

But David knows. David understands, and says, It'll be all right. They're going to Paulie's, but Paulie's isn't Paulie's anymore. It's Mike's.

Same difference, Lynn answers. She doesn't know if that's true, and she hasn't even thought about it. She just speaks, and like that, the world is nothing but runs and puddles until it snaps back into the finest expression of realism. Everything is okay. Everything is just as it seems. Old times.

We've always had, she says, each other.

Paulie's isn't far, and soon, there is the familiar crunch of loose rock under the tires, the same glow of neon in the blue night. It's the time of day when things darken by the second. David parks and cuts the engine. Lynn can hear him breathing. She has the sense that something has gone horribly wrong. Recently. A long time ago. Now. You got the flashlight? she says. She tries to be funny, tries to make what has become an old joke. She can make out his face. She can tell that he's smiling, and not for the first time, she thinks how much he looks like Gary.

Another car pulls up and stops. All the doors pop open, and they seem to pour—the girls—like a stream that bobbles over rocks, like Black Creek itself, the very river Ed champions and pretends to love, a creek Lynn and Gary used to swim, waters that glitter and duck and will pull you down if you aren't careful.

The girls hold each other up as they make their way across the lot, and they are dressed to show. Legs, arms, bellies, and the greater part of chests exposed, and Lynn says, Goodness.

For a minute David says nothing. Lynn watches him watch the girls, and the way he feels isn't perversion so much as a powerful and unusual attraction. This is the way he feels too much, and when David does speak, he says, They're lonely. Everybody can see that.

Lynn looks at the girls. No. They can't.

David breathes and something inside him hums.

When he left, Lynn says, all we had was each other.

The group has gone inside but for one, a girl who stands by the door.

It was more than him, though, Lynn says.

The girl lights a cigarette. She smokes and stands on one foot. She looks out into the lot.

I've been meaning to tell you, Lynn says.

She stops. Behind Paulie's, there's a dark field, a round slope of a thing with just a sliver of night sky that makes a person feel like she's very nearly underground.

She could tell him the truth now. She could tell him about his father, things David has known for years and some things he hasn't.

About those planes, she says. About the one he gave you.

It's special, David says and maybe he's talking about the little Sesna, but he's looking at Paulie's or the girl or the field that's bigger than everything. Special are the certain times, the certain places when and where you can measure the curve of the Earth as clearly as if you were above it. Special is Lynn in the sailor dress and David himself and the picture they make and whatever was and whatever is more than Gary, what only begins with being alone in the world.

It's something else, David says. There isn't a question, but Lynn understands because she's his mother, because she can see things other people can't. She knows more than anything, David wants an answer, and so finally, because she doesn't have her sketchbook, because she can't show him the shape of a person's mouth or the turn of an ear, because too much time has passed, she tries to tell him anything she knows for sure. Yes, she says. It's something else.

RARE AND IMPERILED

She was ashamed to admit it now, but Sarah had thought she'd go inside whatever it was anyway. It wasn't an arena or some kind of center. More like a club, a bar, what—mostly in other countries, she thought—was sometimes still called a discotheque. Lonnie had learned this word in Spanish class. She'd had to write it several times on a worksheet, and when Sarah had seen those letters made by Lonnie's loops and turns, she'd said it herself over and over again. *Discotheque*. Like she couldn't help it, like she was somehow helped *by* it, then and now as she drove the ten miles from the larger town, Florence, to the smaller town, Black Creek, where she and Lonnie and no one else—Sarah remembered, Sarah corrected herself—no one else lived in the house on Quinby Place.

Discoteca. Discoteca. Vamos a la discoteca.

Lonnie must have known all along that Sarah wouldn't be going to the concert, that Lonnie herself wouldn't allow it, and wasn't it strange that your fifteen-year-old daughter would be telling you what you could, and more often could not, do? But this was the way it was or at least the way it was for Sarah and Lonnie.

Every now and then, Sarah would try to take some minor stand usually involving chores, which seemed these days—even though it was just the two of them—to be the bulk of life. You would think, she said or thought she said, we were running a farm.

She tried to be funny, tried to—as her husband might say—take a load off. But then, before she knew it, she was yelling about trash or Lonnie's room or the dishes Lonnie still hadn't washed. Little stuff. Dumb stuff that Sarah didn't really even care about, but lately she found herself in a state of panic. There was a flash of heat and a pounding in her chest. She felt a rush of anxiety that might have taken a much darker form had she not willed herself to focus on the concrete objects before her—the dirty glass, for example, and other things she thought should worry good mothers and good fathers, and she was trying to play both roles now. She was all Lonnie had, and she was yelling from the tops of her lungs until her throat cracked, until Lonnie stormed out and went wherever Lonnie went, places Sarah was sure her daughter would somehow get hurt. Abducted. Killed. Or otherwise lost forever.

All right, Sarah said. It was still daylight when she dropped Lonnie off at the club, just around suppertime— the wrong time, the worst time, Sarah thought, to be in a bar. When the sun showed white and hard every time the door opened. When you were somehow more keenly aware of all the places you weren't—at a table, for instance, eating a meal like a regular person with a regular family. It wouldn't matter if the music was good, only that it was loud enough to drown out your sense of things, and Sarah suspected that even if the music was loud, it wasn't going to be good. Lonnie said the band was getting big, but they weren't the headliners. They weren't even the opening act. They were somewhere high on the card of the club's little festival, but you wouldn't know it to hear Lonnie talk. To hear Lonnie talk was to witness the kind of brittle faith that might also be called denial from a certain perspective.

All right, Sarah said again. The car idled, and she lowered her head to look up at Lonnie through the passenger side window. Sarah, the photographer, should have been interested in that angle, the way the subject appeared larger than she was, but now Sarah, the scared mother, couldn't get past the feeling of being deep below everything. The car seemed to press down upon her with the amazing weight of water or a great mound of dirt, and peering down at her was this giant of a girl who just happened—that's how it felt, that Lonnie just happened to be her daughter. I'll be fine, Sarah said, and when Lonnie didn't hear her, when Sarah had to repeat herself, she added, because a child shouldn't worry whether her mother is fine or not, I'll be at the house.

But now, the house was the last place Sarah wanted to be, and when it came time to turn off the highway which had turned into Main, Sarah kept going. Sarah kept going and then turned down a different street that, if she kept on, would lead her back, a different way to the same town she'd just left. All the roads around here were nothing but circles. So to keep from going where she'd already been, Sarah swerved too fast into the parking lot of the gas station that was also a package store, and in so doing, she nearly hit a woman in jeans who was bending over to pick up what must have been a penny.

The woman kept standing where it wasn't safe to stand, right in the middle of the lot, and hearing the engine and perhaps feeling the heat from it, she straightened and turned, but she didn't stagger backward. She didn't jump out of the way. She stood in the space as if she were a truck or at least the size of one, and she watched the car lurch to a crooked stop in the next space over. She saw the front tires pop the block and then roll back. She blinked when the engine shifted down but kept running.

Inside the car, Sarah uncovered her face. That is, her hand moved from her chapped lips to the base of her neck, and she mouthed, I'm sorry.

The lines around the woman's eyes cinched up, but then so did her chin, and she shook her head. No problem, she said, and through the glass, Sarah was startled to hear the voice, to hear it perfectly fine. Sarah rolled down the window and said, It's been a rough one.

The woman's jaw moved, and she was a series of creases and pocks. She had the kind of face that looked beaten even when it wasn't, but her body had held. Any place else, she might have been fifty. Sixty, even. Here, in Black Creek, the woman could have been thirty-five.

She held up what she'd bent down for, and it wasn't a penny but a bobby pin, and still the woman said, My lucky day.

Inexplicably then, at least it seemed inexplicable to Sarah, the woman stuck out her hand, as if the bobby pin—bent and rusted as it was—were not a bobby pin but some exotic flower, which she tucked, as one would a hibiscus say, above Sarah's ear. Now it's yours, the woman said.

Sarah's first impulse was to recoil, and in fact, she did jump back when she felt the woman's fingers brush against the top of her ear, but she was buckled in the car, and there weren't many places she could go.

The woman was studying her. That's a real pretty dress. Wow-wee.

It was a skirt and an embarrassing one at that—too short, silver sequins of all things. Sarah pulled at it and said, Well. Her finger found the button in the door, and the window went up and might have gone on going up if the woman hadn't lunged forward. Didn't she lunge? But maybe she had only bent down as cool as a car hop with a tray full of French fries and soda pops. Maybe she only leaned closer and said, I've got this real nice top.

Sarah made a sound. A cough. A whimper.

I mean, the woman said, it isn't as pretty as all that.

She had both arms folded across the window, and with a fingernail, she scraped at a scab on her elbow. It's red, and the neck comes down like this. She drew an arrow on her own chest, and then she did a shimmy. Yeah.

Sarah didn't know what to do, so she nodded.

I bet you got a man. She said her man called Howard was there in the store. See him? she said, hitching the strap of her backpack purse. He's in the suit.

And sure enough, there was a hefty little bald man in a gray jacket and gray pants. He stood at the counter, and he had one hand inside his jacket, and the clerk pushed a button, and the register drawer opened, and the clerk handed some money across the counter. Howard didn't move, and the clerk handed him some more.

All right, Sarah said. Her hand was a claw on the door. She felt the bobby pin pulling at her hair.

You wouldn't think it to look at him, the woman said, but she didn't finish. She didn't say what you would think or how it would be wrong.

I better get on, Sarah said.

The engine was still running, and above it, the woman laughed or rather made a kind of hissing sound. You haven't even gone in to get what you came for. You'd give me three guesses, but I only need one.

Sarah shook her head. She told herself she hadn't come here for anything. She'd come here to keep from going anywhere else. She pressed the switch, and the window sprang up another inch, and the woman said, Hey! with such force that Sarah jerked back, and she didn't notice when one of her earrings, a gaudy bobbling thing fell into the floorboard.

The woman's jaw squared. You almost hit me back there, she said, though it wasn't back there at all, but at the very place where the woman still stood big as a truck, now smiling, now showing her gums. You could have killed me.

Sarah opened her mouth. She was suddenly aware of her own teeth, the bulk of them, the way they wanted to chatter.

I think I might be owed, the woman said, and just then, the glass door of the store opened and there on that door were stickers about being eighteen and older, about things that were for sale or else lost, and against this greasy glass and its sad little papers and ghostly fingerprints, there was a string of bells, and the woman sang, In a one-horse open sleigh. Hey! Isn't that right, Howard? Isn't it fun?

And in front of the door which was now closing, the man in the gray suit stood and did not look up at first, as if his name was not Howard at all, and the woman hollered at him. Let's roll. This pretty lady's giving us a ride.

Sarah shook her head, but what she thought was, I don't want to go home. And what she said was *discotheque*, and anyway, it didn't matter what she thought or said or did because here was the woman opening the passenger side door, and here was the woman falling into the seat with her backpack purse and reaching behind her for the belt and clicking it into place as if they all were the best of friends, as if they were setting out for a Saturday morning of shopping or whatever it was people did when they were together, but it wasn't Saturday. It was Friday, and the woman said,

Hurry up. Howard has an appointment. Howard has a very important meeting. Howard! She waved at him until he shoved whatever slip of paper he'd been studying into his jacket pocket and came around and got into the backseat.

They both stared at Sarah until the woman said, Come on then, pretty lady. She tapped the steering wheel. I'll show you where.

≈

In the mirror, Howard's face was backward of what it really must have been—the scar above his eyebrow, the mole on his left cheek, the ear that was just a bit lower—all of this was on the wrong side, but the bottom lip that hung out fat and purple, this could not have been any other way.

The woman had switched on the radio. Playing now was a commercial for artificial knees, a woman carefully detailing the extent of her pain.

Just like my mama, the woman said.

Sarah thought the woman was talking to the radio, that the lady in pain was just like the woman's mama, but the woman pointed at Sarah and said, No. You. You're just like her.

I'm not old enough, Sarah said, to be your mama.

I saw your face, the woman said. I saw that face you made. She turned the dial on the dash until she found a song Sarah didn't know. She didn't know, Lonnie said, any songs. Lonnie said Sarah wouldn't like the concert anyway. And *discotheque*, Lonnie said, was a stupid word.

When a person says something, the woman said, it's decent to say something back.

Sarah blinked. Why?

Because it's manners.

I mean, why am I like your mama? How?

The woman watched Sarah. Then she spoke. Mama never liked playing music in the car. Said you were liable to get hit by a truck. Run over by a train. That happened to somebody she knew. Cut the man's head right off.

Sarah stared at the road.

Because Mama said when you got the radio on you won't hear what's coming next, the woman said. You won't know until it's too late. She reached for the knob, turned it up a few more notches. Howard, you know this song.

The woman had a way. Even when what she said was a question, she wasn't really asking. Sarah, trying it on for herself, said, What's your name?

Still her voice lifted and shook just like it did when she yelled at Lonnie, as if something inside were rattling and might, at any moment, turn loose.

Tarja, the woman said.

Tarja, Sarah said. Something in the mirror, a car, caught her eye.

Yeah. What about it?

Nothing.

You don't like it.

I like it. It's nice.

Nice.

It's pretty is what I mean. It's a real pretty name.

Tarja's eyes were on Sarah. She considered. She searched. Then finally, she smiled. Finally, she showed the gums that were mostly pink but also in some places white. It is pretty, she said, even if nobody thinks so.

Sarah nodded and blinked. She checked the mirror. In the backseat, Howard pointed at something. He pressed his finger to the glass. His purple lip moved, but he said nothing.

Is he okay? Sarah said.

Tarja looked at the road in front of them. Just drive.

They were passing the last of what, in Black Creek, amounted to subdivisions—Wessex, King's Gate, the Country Club Estates. They were coming up on the turnoff, which they might have gone down had they been turning back toward the town where Lonnie was. Thinking of Lonnie, Sarah let her foot off the gas, but Lonnie didn't want her around. She'd made that clear, and Tarja said, Keep going.

And so they did. They kept going past all the metal buildings. Sarah didn't know what they were, but they seemed to be all around Black Creek, a kind of corrugated moat of disrepair and neglect.

And past all this, far away from anything, so far that from the inside, you felt as if you were on another planet was a nowhere entirely. There were flashing lights, the ambulances, the hospital with that name Carolina Pines that was meant to make you think of a forest and the birds in the branches. Maybe there were only some like Sarah who thought that Carolina Pines sounded more like a place where things crawled to die.

When it finally happened, John's feet had slipped from underneath the sheet. He'd been at the hospital for nearly a month, and without thinking, without hesitation, Sarah reached to tuck the blanket up under his heels, the heels she'd rubbed with lotion not two hours earlier. In that moment, she thought only of chill and always the desire, the need to be warm. But it wasn't always, this necessity. It wasn't even close.

Before Lonnie was born, they'd had a dog named Chipper, an old Basset that John had in high school and later in college. Chipper was thirteen years old, blind and septic when he disappeared. The woods, John said. That's where he's gone, and he nodded in the direction of Black Creek Park where—before he got so bad—they used to take Chipper for walks.

Sarah had wanted to go looking right then—He's blind! she'd said because Sarah, who spent most of those days looking through a lens or staring down into a developing tray, could not imagine navigating a world thrown into total darkness—but John had stopped her. John had taken her arm and said sometimes it was best to let things pass their own way.

Still Sarah had loved Chipper, and when John went to work, she put on her boots and went down to the park, down to the creek. She'd searched everywhere, even under logs where she knew Chipper couldn't be, and in the process, she'd found a stash of beer bottles and a spiral notebook the rain washed out, but she'd never found the dog. She walked those paths until it was nearly dark, until she knew John would be home soon.

Down there, beside the water, she could barely hear the cars on the street. She and John often said how peaceful it was, and she wondered if peace was what Chipper was after. Or privacy. Or was it something else? Something you wouldn't recognize until you saw it, until you felt it for yourself. Something the dog had heard calling to him.

In that room, that window, fifth from the end. While Lonnie had studied for her Spanish test, all the words for all the places. *Iglesia. Parque. Discoteca.* A stupid word they shouldn't have to learn, Lonnie said. Disco, Lonnie said, is dead.

She'd always say a prayer, too, Tarja said. Mama would. Just like that. Just like you. Whenever we saw an ambulance.

Sarah opened her mouth, and Tarja said, This hair. She grabbed her purse. She unzipped the front pocket and took out a plastic comb that was just like the combs the schools gave children so they could fix themselves before Sarah took their pictures. Those were the only photographs she took anymore. Sometimes as many as 400, 500 shots in a single day. When she closed her eyes at night, when she tried to sleep, she saw their faces, and what might have brought joy to some now only inspired in Sarah a special kind of horror. She'd wake up in a sweat, nearly screaming. She'd go check on Lonnie, make sure she was all right.

Tarja was dragging the comb through her hair. Every time we heard a siren, Mama started talking to Jesus. She said you never knew when it might be you. I guess, Tarja said, it's always somebody.

In the backseat, Howard had a hand inside his coat. He might have been clutching his chest or something else he had in the pocket.

You don't care if he cracks the window, Tarja said. Then to Howard: Crack the window. Get some air.

Into the car, there came a loud rush. He needs some wind, Tarja said. His mind is playing tricks, telling him we're not moving. Howard, we're moving.

It had been a while since Sarah had driven out past the hospital. I don't know where to go, she said.

Not much farther, Tarja said. The comb snagged in a tangle, and one of the teeth broke.

I mean, Sarah said, as Tarja ripped at her hair, where are we going?

I told you I'd tell you, Tarja said. Her voice was sharp, and her body moved with a terrible quickness. She bent down to the floorboard, and when she straightened up, she had a gun, and she was aiming it at Sarah, and she was pulling the trigger, and there were pieces of Sarah's skull stuck to the glass, which was shattered rather beautifully, and Sarah saw all of this in the mind that was most certainly in the next few seconds about to go as dark as dark can be, and she was actually steeled against this. She was actually squinting even as she drove, even as she realized that nothing had happened and what Tarja held was not a gun, but Sarah's very own earring, or rather, Lonnie's earring that Sarah had borrowed because her own weren't right. Her own weren't right, and she'd borrowed these from Lonnie, and even then, Lonnie hadn't said anything. Only later, when they were driving up to the place, to the concert, did Lonnie say, You don't need to be here.

Pretty, Tarja said. She held the earring up and out. It would be nighttime soon, but now, the late afternoon sun made of the imitation jewels a kind of miniature stained glass. In one second, Tarja was staring at the earring. In the next second, she was looking past it at Sarah. And in the next, she was threading the earring, as fast as one might thread a fishing hook, with the flap of her own ear. I'm always finding stuff, she said. People lose everything.

From the backseat, there came a long, low moan.

He's sick, Sarah said.

He's all right. Tarja turned back, and the earring swung against a green bruise on her neck. Howard's all right. Yeah, Howard is.

Sarah thought again of Chipper—all the names they'd called him. Chips. Chipster. Chippy-Dippy.

Almost there, Tarja said. I see the turnoff.

Where? Sarah said.

Tarja didn't answer until they went up and over a rise and then around a corner, and then finally she said, Up here. Yeah. There.

Sarah's foot moved from the gas to the brake. She turned on the blinker. She drove with a student's exaggerated focus and precision, as though she were trying to pass a test. She made the turn down the dirt road under the sign that said Lake Darpo.

≈

An ugly lake—dark and treacherous. Lake Darpo was a dammed tributary of Black Creek and just the kind of place for children to drown, which they did—one or two every year despite all the signs that said SWIM AT YOUR OWN RISK.

At Lake Darpo, risk, one dumb cop joked, is anything but a game. An unfortunate quote reported by Black Creek's local newspaper. The next week, that same cop issued a public apology, which John had read out loud during breakfast. Everybody knew kids dying wasn't funny. Humor, the cop wrote, is a crude coping mechanism. But as an officer of the law, as a person more generally, you had to cope. You had to survive. You had to somehow get through.

He's right about that, John said. We don't have a choice.

Sarah was chewing her toast. She could feel it cutting her mouth. There's always a choice, she said.

Darpo was an acronym that ended in police officers, but Sarah could never keep the rest straight. The lake belonged to law enforcement, but anybody could come for the day. Every year, there was a big duck hunt. Ducks, mallards mostly, were hauled in from elsewhere, fed for a few weeks, then shot and hung by their feet. Here, too, was a stand of long-leaf pines and a few supposed sightings of the rare and imperiled red-cockaded woodpecker. They were already extinct in Maryland, Missouri, and New Jersey. The Black Creek sightings needed to be confirmed. A description of the precise location and habitat. A photo. Some proof of life. Then there would be some changes at Lake Darpo. Some effort toward conservation.

Sarah had come out here once, she and John. For their anniversary.

Going to the lake had been Sarah's idea. What she wanted was to get out of the doctor's office. I want to see, she said, something besides X-rays.

She'd told John about the ducks, about the woodpeckers. What else is out there? he said. He was teasing her. Bigfoot? Loch Ness?

Maybe, Sarah said, not knowing what exactly they might see, only that it was important to look.

But that day, the lake and, it seemed, the very air she and John breathed was perforated with the sound of gunshots. Pop, pop, pop, pop, pop. More than one at a time, and more than Sarah could count. Her first thought was that someone was being killed. This was always her first thought after John's diagnosis, which that particular anniversary had been—four months after, to be exact.

John was young, the doctors said. He still seemed all right then, like maybe there was some chance. That was before they knew it had spread.

It was John who figured out by some mysterious set of signs and clues that cops used part of the park as a shooting range. Probably the safest place in town, he said, and he put his arm around Sarah, and he looked okay, but his hand was cold, and soon he started coughing, and Sarah didn't feel safe. No matter how hard she tried, when a gun was fired, she couldn't keep from jumping.

That was a year ago now. No, Sarah realized. It was more than a year. Even the playground equipment and the basketball goals and the picnic tables seemed more rusted, broken in new ways. The whole place was falling in on itself, and this time, when Sarah pulled up in the lot and cut the engine, there were no gunshots. There was only one other car, a Crown Victoria, in the lot.

It's late for appointments, Sarah said. She'd thought about this earlier. She'd noticed, too, that even though the clerk seemed to be making change, Howard, like her, hadn't bought anything at the store.

I told you we've got business, Tarja said. You don't think we have business?

I didn't say that.

Tarja looked at her.

I think you've got business, Sarah said.

We've got some things to settle, Tarja said.

Sarah nodded.

In the backseat, Howard sat still, but his fat lip quivered.

Tarja stared hard at Sarah. Stay here, she said and un-buckled her safety belt. She got out of the car and shut the door. Then she opened Howard's. Come on now. You've done good so far.

Finally, Howard moved. He swung one leg out and then the other. At the convenience store, Tarja had seemed tall and strong. Actually, she wasn't that big at all. She probably wasn't much taller than Lonnie, and still Howard was shorter than her, by nearly a foot.

Tarja licked her finger and rubbed at the corner of his mouth. She said something Sarah couldn't hear. In the mirror, she saw Tarja's hand on Howard's chest.

Right up there, Tarja said and pointed to the back side of small brick building that sat up on a weedy hill. She pushed Howard in the general direction. When he stopped and looked back at her, she said, Go on, and he did. He went on.

Tarja scratched her arms. She watched for some minutes until Howard disappeared around the corner of the building. Then she turned around. Her face was blank, and enough time passed for Sarah to wonder what exactly Tarja planned to do.

Then Tarja reached down into the floorboard of the backseat. When she straightened up, she had Sarah's camera bag. She was unzipping it, pulling out the Nikon, saying, Wow-wee, pretty lady. She held the camera up to her face and pointed it at Sarah.

Careful, Sarah said.

And Tarja said, It's expensive.

It's important, Sarah said, but she didn't believe it. Not anymore. At the last minute, she'd grabbed the camera thinking she might take some pictures at the concert. She thought she might get some good shots of Lonnie.

Come on, Tarja said, and now she did open the door. Come on and take my picture.

Tarja was already walking toward the water. The camera bounced on her chest.

Sarah watched her through the windshield. Then she unfastened her belt and got out of the car. She looked up at the trees. She looked at the trees across the water.

There she is, John had said, pointing at two stumps in the middle of the lake. There's our Nessie.

There's no such thing, Sarah said, rolling her eyes. But the truth was she hoped they would see something. She hoped they'd *feel* something just as miraculous, just as— she thought now—stupid.

Her legs were moving, and when she caught up, Tarja took the camera off and slipped the strap over Sarah's head. The weight of it surprised Sarah, the heft that snapped against her neck. Over here, Tarja said. She went over to a big rock. She leaned up against it with her head back and her hips thrust out, a pin-up imitation so poor that Tarja herself must have sensed it because just as quickly, she went limp and, frowning, said, I need a smoke.

Sarah's fingers moved on the dials of the camera.

The car, Tarja said. I smelled it.

Sarah held the camera over her face. They're gone.

Tarja seemed to mull this over. It's a nice car.

It's a Honda.

Tarja nodded.

Sarah lowered the camera.

What? Tarja said.

And Sarah shook her head. Sarah shook her head quick. Nothing, she said. She tucked her hair behind her ear, felt the bobby pin still in her hair. Sit back up there, she said, pointing her chin at the rock. But face the water.

Tarja blinked at Sarah. Then she did what Sarah said. But as soon as Sarah held up the camera, Tarja turned and sucked in her gut and smiled.

Not like that, Sarah said. Just look at the water. Pretend I'm not here.

Tarja's smile faded, and there was something else—a flash of anger? embarrassment?—but she turned her head. She looked away.

Tell me something, Sarah said. It was an old trick, a way to relax a person, to distract from what was really going on. Tell me something else about your mother.

Tarja snorted. Like what?

I don't know. Something. Don't look at me, she said. Look at the water.

Tarja watched Sarah. Her eyes lifted to the hill, to the little brick house. But then, she turned back. The last of the sun made light of her face.

Tell me how y'all were, Sarah said.

Tarja licked her lips. How we were, was happy as wet cats. Her hair was wild again and she pushed it back off her face. There was the bruise, Lonnie's earring, sharp pieces of glass. I used to drive my mama crazy.

Sarah took a couple of shots. She adjusted the knobs, took a couple more.

I was always asking her why Jesus didn't talk to me like he talked to her. I was worried, you know. That I wasn't praying right or something.

It had been a long time since Sarah had taken these kinds of pictures. The first shots wouldn't be any good. Sarah knew that, but she took a few steps closer, tried again.

Tarja kept talking. Mama said there wasn't no right or wrong way. She said you just talk.

Sarah got closer. Her skirt was shining, casting points of light across Tarja's back.

When you talk to Jesus, Tarja said, you just say whatever needs saying.

Through the lens, or maybe it was in that light, Tarja looked different—younger, closer to Lonnie's age than Sarah's.

So I kept saying whatever, Tarja said. I kept doing just what Mama said, and I kept praying, and I kept listening.

Sarah was very close behind Tarja now. She might have reached out and pushed her right off the rock. She let loose of the camera. She had what she needed. Did you hear something? Sarah said, and Tarja's head swung around. She didn't know Sarah had gotten so close. She wiped at her face, and it changed then, back to the way it was in the lot, and she said, You're tricking me.

There at the lake, on their anniversary, Sarah had tried to tease John back. Shut up, she said when he kidded her about the monsters. There's no such thing. She pushed him, but she should have pushed him harder because maybe there was. Maybe more was possible than any of them knew, and maybe it wasn't all bad.

You think I'm stupid, Tarja said. She stood up on the rock, and she was tall now. She was taller than any person could be. You think I don't know what you're doing.

Sarah should have kicked John. She should have punched him in the face, and Sarah saw Tarja well enough now but she also saw John and, for the first time in a long time, she saw, she looked hard at that part of herself. She felt the rush, the pump in her chest, and it was fear. Sure, it was. But there was something else, too, and Sarah knew it. She saw then how this could turn out, what she might do. She saw the fear, and she saw what might be on the other side.

But there, in the middle distance, was the sound and the report, and she and Tarja drew back at the same time, as if they were two parts of a whole, a pair of awkward, delicate wings. And Sarah had spent her whole life looking, and now she'd finally seen some things, but what mattered most was what she heard, what she had been hearing—the beating of her own blood now all around them, a persistent knocking and then the flail and the flutter that could only be a kind of wonder startled into flight.

SISTERS

It didn't matter what her sister said, Lucy was on her way to Black Creek.

Ann needed help after the baby. That was a simple fact, and for once, Lucy meant to do the exact right thing. Maybe I'll try being perfect for a change, she said into the phone.

She meant to be funny, but Ann didn't laugh. She shouldn't have said it any more than she should have told the stranger on the plane where she was headed. Lucy's mouth was always getting her in trouble. She didn't think before she talked, and that's why, Ann said, she was always getting her ass in a crack.

My sister Ann, she said as she fumbled for the seat belt. She needs help after the baby.

The stranger was an old woman with hair that was not quite gray and not quite yellow. Pinned on the collar of her blouse was a beetle made of green and purple costume jewels. A strand of hot glue moved in the plane's conditioned air. The stranger cooed like a bird. Isn't that nice? Girl or baby boy?

Lucy hadn't meant to say what she said, or at least she hadn't meant to stop. She'd only hesitated, considering how best to tell the truth. But in the pause, the half-lie formed, and when the stranger looked at her through rheumed eyes, the correction didn't seem worth the effort.

A girl, she said.

The old woman smacked and clucked. Girls are a trial.

Lucy smiled. They were up in the air now, and in that new pressure, the woman had a hard time hearing. Lucy tried to say something, but she just patted a floppy ear and shook her head.

A dingy haze moved past the window. Down below, Lucy could see the city, cars snarled in traffic. She wrapped the hem of her shirt around her finger. She wondered how long before the drink cart.

Only a few minutes passed before she felt the weight of the stranger's head. The woman had been thumbing through *OK!* magazine, and held it still, even as she nodded off. She was a small woman, but the head on Lucy's shoulder was tremendously heavy and seemed to get heavier by the second.

Lucy stared down at the woman's hair, at the bald spot the woman could not see to fluff and cover. She was staring at this hole, at this patch of pink skin when she jerked her shoulder and shifted away.

The woman stirred but didn't wake. Her chin rested on her chest. She must have been in her eighties. The way she slept, she might have been dead. Certainly, she would be soon. Lucy watched. Somewhere in the back, there was the rattle of ice, the crink of plastic. Lucy tried to swallow and couldn't. Her mouth was dry, and the old woman next to her went blurry.

≈

I would have walked right past you, Ann said.

They were driving the twelve miles from the regional airport to Black Creek. The road was smooth, but Lucy gripped at the passenger side door. The sisters hadn't seen each other in more than two years.

You look, Ann said, different.

Thanks, Lucy said. I think.

Ann seemed like she might smile, but she scratched her face instead.

The car wasn't new, but it was vacuumed and dusted. The engine was quiet. A man was talking on the radio. The volume was turned too low to hear anything specific.

I wanted to tell you in person, Lucy said. I'm sorry.

What? Ann said. She looked at Lucy. Oh, right.

Ann turned her focus back to the road. They were coming up on one of the developments. Against the low sun, the wooden frame of a house turned black, and the boards stood out like bones.

Every time I come this way, Ann said, there's another one where I least expect it.

Lucy's head bobbed.

A lot's changed, she said, but you wouldn't know it.

What Ann said was true. Lucy wouldn't know the difference. This was her first time coming to Black Creek.

I knew you, Lucy said. You look just the same.

There was a cat in the ditch, and Ann saw it but didn't brake. No, I don't.

≈

When Rob and Ann first got together, seven years ago now, Lucy couldn't get over the fact that Rob was a traveling salesman. She couldn't believe that such a person still existed, and even now, Rob seemed like a phantom, some character Ann had seen in an old Turner Classic. He was never home, and he wasn't now, and Ann said she couldn't really remember where he was—California or Oregon or somewhere over there. She gestured vaguely. I don't keep it straight, she said.

Primarily, he sold clocks—expensive exact clocks to schools and jails and hospitals, places where time really mattered.

When's he coming back? Lucy said.

A few days. A week maybe.

Ann was carrying Lucy's bag into the house, and even when Lucy tried to wrestle it from her, Ann jerked away, said, I got it.

But—Lucy said.

I'm fine, Ann said, and Lucy knew better than to argue.

Like Ann's car, the house wasn't new. In fact, like almost all the houses in the neighborhood, it was more than a hundred years old, but the floors were redone, the windows were new, and Ann kept the place spotless. It smelled like lemons and floor wax, and when Ann opened the bedroom door, there was the heavy smell of fresh paint.

Ann set Lucy's bag on the floor. So you can stay in here.

She looked down at the bed, and though the comforter was clean and laid flat, Ann slapped at it, hard, as if to shake something loose. When she turned back, Lucy tried to stand straighter. She held up her chin.

You probably want to rest, Ann said.

Something to drink?

Water.

Lucy nodded.

Ann pointed toward the bathroom. There's towels in the cabinet. Soap and all.

Right, Lucy said. She waited for Ann to say something else, but instead Ann moved toward the door.

I'm happy, Lucy started and then stopped. Her voice sounded so loud. She was yelling even though Ann was just out of arm's reach. She tried again. I'm glad I'm here.

Ann stood there. Her head might have moved or maybe it was only a muscle flinching. I'll make us some soup, she said, and then she pulled the door shut behind her.

Lucy was alone in the room. She looked at the new white walls, at a patched place where something had hung. She wanted to take a bath, but instead, she was pushing off her shoes. She was lying back on the bed. She was pleating the edge of the bedspread as was her nervous habit. There was something hard there beneath her thumb. She pulled the fabric closer and saw it was the plastic cord that held the tag. She ran the plastic up under her nail. She drove it down until it hurt, and in the changed evening light, she believed she could see the walls turn the faintest shade of pink.

≈

Why do they do that? Lucy said.

It was the next morning. She'd fallen asleep the night before, and when she woke up, it was nearly eleven o'clock at night. Ann was in her bedroom with the door shut. In the kitchen, Lucy found a ham sandwich mummified in Saran wrap and a bag of potato chips on the counter. Soup's in the fridge, a note said.

Now they were sitting at the dining table drinking coffee and watching the brown birds that kept throwing themselves up against the bay windows. They're hurting themselves, Lucy said.

Ann held her coffee cup. I guess they'll learn. Or they won't.

Lucy stared at the window. Maybe you could get one of those owls, she said. The kind that scares things away.

Ann took a drink. Maybe, she said.

The bird hooked his claws in the screen. He turned his head, and Lucy could see the black eye jerking.

Lucy blinked like she might fall back asleep. I was just thinking, she said, about Mama wearing all those awful wigs.

The bird tapped its beak, like a thin fingernail, against the window.

She had cancer, Ann said.

That red one, Lucy said as if Ann had said nothing at all, was the worst.

The bird flapped its wings and flew away.

She did the best she could, Ann said.

Let's go someplace, Lucy said.

Ann set down her coffee cup. There were red and green cows painted on the side. I'm not going to a bar with you.

I'm not talking about a bar. Who said anything about a bar?

Ann looked up at her.

I'm talking about outside. It's a nice day.

Ann turned her head. Her skin was very pale, and around her nose, it was flaking in rough raw patches. I don't know.

There's got to be some place, Lucy said.

There's the park.

The park, Lucy said, and she actually clapped her hands. Ann jumped. Perfect. The park.

≈

The park was more than seventy acres of cypress forest located in the floodplain of Black Creek. Most of the park was swampland that, on account of the mosquitoes, was unbearable during the summer months, but now, in December, there had been a frost that killed almost everything.

You must come here a lot, Lucy said. She was trying to keep up, but Ann was moving fast.

Not really, Ann said. She trudged ahead.

Lucy heard something above them. She was looking up at a bird in the sky—a hawk—when Ann slipped on some leaves. Lucy saw her reach out and grab at the air. Ann tried and failed to catch her balance, and before she could do anything else, she landed hard on the damp ground.

Lucy rushed to catch up. She was asking what happened, was Ann okay, was anything broken, what could she do?

Nothing, Ann said. I'm fine. Just tripped is all.

Here, Lucy said. She grabbed Ann's arm, but Ann shook her off. Let me help.

Don't, Ann snapped. You can't.

Lucy had crouched over Ann, but now she took a step back. Her mouth was open, but she said nothing.

I'm too heavy, Ann said. Then she pushed herself up off the ground and dusted her pants. You wanted to get out. So, she gestured for Lucy to walk in front, get out.

Don't do that, Lucy said.

Do what? We're doing what you want just like always.

Lucy stood in the trail, but Ann brushed past her, spinning her around. What you're doing, Lucy said, and she worked her way to yelling because Ann was getting further and further away. What you're doing is playing tough.

Ann stopped. The seat of her pants was filthy with leaves and mud. She turned around, pointed at Lucy, and said, The only person who ever gets to play anything is you.

Above them, the hawk whistled. The hawk whistled and circled.

That's, Lucy faltered. That's just—crap, and you know it.

But Ann was already moving down the trail, and Lucy should have run to keep up with her, but she was scared, and so instead, she did a kind of stutter step. Ann, she said, not unlike she'd said so often as a kid when Ann ran away from her. Ann, wait up!

They were coming up on the creek and a wooden plank bridge that arched up and over the water.

Ann had been marching along, but now that she got to the bridge, she slowed and finally stopped. She seemed to glance over the side of the bridge, and a hand drew up and covered her mouth, then moved to her belly. She sort of staggered backward, hunched over herself.

Ann? Lucy said. Annie?

Something was wrong, and Lucy ran now. She ran the rest of the trail, and though her feet slid under her, she kept her balance and kept on, and when she hit the boarded bridge, it was with the force and the weight of a spurred horse. Ann. Annie, I'm here.

Lucy reached out toward Ann's belly. It hadn't been that long—a few weeks since the baby. Since the last baby. Ann was older. There could still be complications. Cramps. Pain. Hemorrhages. Lucy just touched Ann's hand, which was cold and dry, but Ann waved her off. Ann gestured as she had when talking about Rob. Over there, she'd said. Somewhere. But now, she meant over the side of the bridge, in the water.

What? Lucy said. Though she knew it must be something, she couldn't see it just yet, and from the look on Ann's face, she might never want to see it, but still, like the girl in the horror movie who opens the door, who goes in the barn, who takes the first step down the stairs toward the basement, so often in life it seemed to Lucy that despite what Ann thought, she rarely had any choice. Life, for Lucy, was a series of compulsions, and even though stepping forward would become so much more than an urge or an impulse, it was, in that moment, that simple. A force and an action on that force, and she was taking a step forward, and she was looking down, and she was seeing the girl under the water.

≈

Both women had cell phones in their pockets, but Ann reached for hers first. She dialed 9-1-1. She listened to the line ring twice. When a voice said, What is your emergency?, she stuck a finger in her other ear, and said, Yes, my name is Ann Murfin. I'm with my sister, Lucy, at Black Creek Park, and we've just found a girl. A body.

But no. This was not what happened. This was what Lucy saw in her mind, what she expected before the phone dropped from Ann's shaking hands, and it was so long, it seemed, that the phone hung in the air and above them, the hawk still whistled, and Ann's mouth hung open, and Lucy reached for the phone, but her arms were heavy and like everything, so slow, and then it hit the boards with a racket that made Lucy shake her head.

We've got, she said, to do something.

This was the part when Ann should have said just exactly what they should do, or—more often—she was already doing it, but now she just stood there, frozen in time, and some part of Lucy's mind flashed to an exhibit she'd seen in San Francisco, the people of Pompeii, eyes and mouths agape at what could only be described as awesome—dread, veneration, wonder.

She did not feel like herself but rather an imperson- ation of Ann as she dialed the number, as she answered the questions, as she described the situation. But still, it was her finger. It was her voice. It was her name she gave the woman on the other end of the line.

Police are on their way, the woman said, and Lucy said, Okay, thank you. She ended the call. She thought to hand the phone back to Ann, but instead, stuck it in her own pocket. Ann, she said, are you hurt?

Ann's eyes fluttered. She was very pale, and Lucy thought she would say yes, that she was hurt. She was, in fact, hurt very badly, but after a minute, Ann shook her head. She stared at the body, and Lucy said, Come on. Let's go over here.

She tried to steer Ann away, but Ann said no. Her voice was a burst, a puncture in the woods. I'm staying, she said, more quietly.

All right, Lucy said. Okay. She reached out. Under her hand, she felt the bones of Ann's back. She felt the quick rise and fall of her breathing. In the distance, a siren.

≈

A few days passed. They identified the girl but would not release her name. She was a minor, they said. They were working to contact her parents. The supposed cause of death was drowning, though, the coroner allowed, it was difficult to say whether it was accidental or not. If someone else was involved. Or not. A full autopsy was pending.

Lucy sat at the dining room table. She read the article out loud. When she finished, she looked over the top of the newspaper. Ann was in the armchair in the living room. It was almost noon, but she was still in her bathrobe. She was staring out the window.

Lucy held the newspaper. Then she folded it, placed it on the table. I think those birds have quit, she said. They just gave up.

The house was so quiet, Lucy could hear it settling beneath them. Somewhere a clock ticked. You want to turn on the TV?

Then Ann said, I'd like some flowers. I'd like some flowers to take.

Lucy looked at her. She watched her. She saw, in Ann, their mother. She saw time passing. She said, I'll drive.

≈

They weren't the only ones. It seemed that all of Black Creek had thought to bring flowers or stuffed animals or candles with the names of saints. The little wooden bridge, carved with the names of lovers and curses and numbers to call, had turned into a kind of shrine. An old woman left just as Lucy and Ann arrived, and then they were alone. They sat down on the bridge, and for a long while, they were quiet. For a long while, there was only the sound of the water passing beneath them.

The candles burned and most were saints in various poses of pain and affliction, but one showed Mother Mary herself. She wore the blue and white cloak, and her arms opened toward them, and Lucy thought of the girl. The creek was just the creek again, as if the girl had never been there, as if she were some sort of apparition, a fleeting vision.

I never saw her, a voice said, and at first, Lucy took it for a stranger talking about the girl in the river. The voice was so unsteady, so uncertain, she wouldn't have known it for Ann's except she saw her now. She saw her speaking. They wouldn't let me, she said, and her hand was on her belly. They said there was nothing to see.

Lucy opened her mouth and shut it again. Most of her life, she'd wanted Ann to talk to her, to open up like other sisters she knew, and now that it was happening, she didn't know what to say or how to act. She couldn't even look at Ann, and so she stared at the candle, at Mother Mary, and the flickering flame that seemed as out of balance as everything else. Finally, she said, It happens more than we know. Women just don't talk—

Because what good does it do? Ann said, and her voice was her own again. Lucy would have known that edge anywhere. Words don't change things.

What I mean is, Lucy said, forcing herself to look at Ann, I'm here.

Ann blinked. She snorted, and her lip flapped. No, you aren't.

Lucy studied her sister. She wanted to argue, to say that Ann was wrong, that they had each other, but there was a dull certainty in Ann's eye, a confidence that could not be swayed, and, in fact, made Lucy wonder if this was another time when Ann knew something she didn't.

Lucy turned back to the water. Night came faster to the swamp. Already, it was getting dark, and off in the woods, a flash caught Lucy's eye.

She drew in a sharp breath and without thinking, she grabbed for Ann's hand. You see that?

Ann sniffed. She squinted at the lengthening shadows. What?

Lucy searched the woods. Whatever she'd seen was gone. There aren't wolves here, she said. Right?

Ann shook her head. Must have been something else, she said, but she kept looking in the trees.

Yeah. Must have been.

Lucy had grabbed Ann's hand, but Ann held on, and they stayed like this until there was almost no light left.

THERE YOU ARE

In the first place, Jill didn't want the baby, and this surprised everyone except for Jill. I never wanted kids, she told Cathy, and this wasn't exactly true, but it was true enough.

Even some of their closest friends couldn't understand. When Jill complained about the baby crying or spitting up on itself or pooping its diaper again, they gaped at her like she was some sort of monster. They told her she couldn't keep calling the baby *it*. That's how kids develop complexes, they said. That's why they grow up and kill their teachers.

Jill had heard the word *complex*, but she wasn't exactly clear on what it meant. It made her think about apartments, and apartments reminded her of a sticky hive crawling with thousands of buzzing bees.

How come, Jill said, you never hear about teachers killing kids?

They—Cathy and the friends—thought this was terrible, too. What was wrong with Jill? How did she come up with this stuff?

Rampaging teachers. Apartments and bees and walls made of wax. Complexes. Jill wondered if she had one.

Just now, she was painting her nails Blue Blazes. Her hands shook as they had since junior high, but the tremors were getting worse. She had to plant her palm against the stained arm of the recliner to have any hope at all, and even then, the brush trembled and bobbed. She might have dipped the tip of her finger into the bottle and got a similar, perhaps better, result.

Porky the Parrot watched from Jill's shoulder. You're too sexy, he said. You're too sexy for your clothes.

The television was on—some kid show with lots of music. Cathy was dressed for work, but she was on the floor with Barbara, wincing as she shifted from one bad knee to the other. Barbara couldn't stand up on her own, so Cathy held her little hands and bobbed her own head in a kind of dance.

Cathy blew air from between her lips. She opened her eyes and her mouth wide. Then she strung a bunch of nonsense sounds together, and smiled at Barbara as if, in the middle of their baby conversation, one of them had told a smart joke.

You're too sexy for your hat, Porky said, and Jill said, Goddammit, because she'd jumped when Porky brushed against her ear. His wing was light, like nothing at all, like air, like breath against Jill's skin, and now there was an ugly streak of blue down her pinky finger all the way to the knuckle.

Ha-HA, Cathy said. HA-ha, HA-ha, ha!

Jill glared, but Cathy was making faces at the baby. They'd had Barbara for nearly a month, but Jill still wasn't used to it. She felt like she was always trying to guess who was talking to who. Cathy said something else, and when Jill didn't respond, Cathy said, Anybody home?

What? Jill said. Me?

I said, she'll be walking any day now.

Barbara squealed as if she understood. She held tight to Cathy's fingers. Her dimpled knees buckled in and out and in again.

See? Cathy said.

Whatchya think about that? Porky said and jumped on top of Jill's head. Think about that, whatchya.

Cathy's talkie squawked. She pulled it from her belt and adjusted the volume.

Barbara frowned and reached for the talkie. She missed and, off balance, sat back hard on her diapered bottom. She looked like she might cry. From the radio came a string of words and numbers, codes.

Cathy's face was grim as she clipped the talkie back to her belt. The navy EMS shirt and the cargo pants made Jill think of the military. There she goes, Jill said, reporting for duty. She meant to be funny. The parrot said something that didn't mean anything.

We should watch how we talk, Cathy said, in front of the baby.

Cathy stood and swung Barbara up on her shoulder in one fluid motion as if she'd been doing such a thing all her life. Another wreck, she said. Out toward Darpo.

I didn't say anything, Jill said.

Cathy pressed her lips against Barbara's sticky cheek.

Porky just scared me. That's all.

Cathy sat the baby down in Jill's lap. She gets what you're saying. She gets a lot more than you know.

Barbara squirmed in Jill's lap. She made a face. Jill held her wet nails in the air. She opened her mouth to say something, and Cathy kissed her on the cheek. BRB, she said, and in a rattle of keys and boot stomps, she was gone.

Usually, Cathy worked the night shift so that when Jill was alone with the baby, most often they both just slept. Sometimes Barbara cried, and Jill would wake up and lie there listening. It was a lonely suffering sound, like a dog or something wilder, and Jill would think of her brother Boone, those times he'd go hunting and miss the clean shot. All night, she'd hear the rabbit, and sometimes she'd find its blood trail, the quiet places it dragged itself to hurt in some sort of peace.

Jill told herself that if Barbara's crying went on long enough, she'd go check. But eventually, Barbara seemed to whimper herself to sleep, and the next thing Jill knew, she was waking up again, and Cathy was back. Time, since Jill had moved in with Cathy and particularly since they got Barbara, seemed to move differently. Through one of the windows upstairs, Jill sometimes saw the sun in one corner of the sky and a piece of the moon in the other. It wasn't right to see both at once. She'd never thought so. It made a person feel like she was on an altogether different planet, and there were times when Jill was so tired she wouldn't have been the least bit surprised to find her feet floating up off the ground, to find herself slipping up through the top of the house and the sky and the atmosphere which supposedly kept the world from bursting into flames.

You didn't hear about teachers killing kids, but the same couldn't be said for mothers.

Barbara squirmed, and she might have fell over backward if Jill hadn't caught her. Jill kept her from falling, but she held the baby too tight. She felt the soft baby flesh and soft baby bones against the muscles and the points of her own arms.

Barbara let out a wail, a rabbit missing two of her feet, a ragged hole for an ear. Barbara flashed the few teeth she'd grown, and Jill said, Stop it. Just quit already.

Outside, the dog barked, and Porky hollered, You're so sexy. You're so sexy it hurts!

≈

Barbara's daddy was Cathy's nephew, and at first, Jill didn't think he was intellectually disabled, but now she wasn't so sure. He'd come by the house twice since she and Cathy had been keeping the baby, and both times, he'd sat on the couch like a lug with his oily black hair over his eyes, and his mouth hanging open until Jill could see the only glimmer of anything about him—a small bubble of spit at the corner of his pale, chapped lips.

He was sixteen years old, and it was a miracle and a mystery how and why anyone had ever slept with him, but someone had, presumably. Cathy said the girl's name was Nicole.

Who is she? Jill said. Where does she work? What does she do?

And the nephew, sunk even deeper into the crevices of the couch, muttered something Jill had to ask him to repeat.

Ralphie's, he said.

It was unclear which, if any, of Jill's questions the nephew was answering, but at the time, Jill couldn't muster the energy to pry anything else out of him, and now it was all the information she had—Ralphie's Roller Rama. She would go there. She would take Barbara back where she belonged. Jill had to do this before she did something else.

Jill drove around the square in the only direction that was legal, the streets around the courthouse being their own kind of rink where people routinely cut each other off and stopped in the middle of the road to wait on a good parking spot. Jill lived in Columbia for a while (She always said South Carolina, not South America until she realized people were laughing at her. Of course, it was South Carolina.), and it drove her crazy how country people drove any which way they wanted and at their own pace. Even now, as the Cutlass in front of Jill hesitated ever so slightly at the recently turned-green light, Jill laid on her horn and yelled, Come on!

She was in some kind of hurry.

The Roller Rama was about a mile down Vine Street. The cement block building, formerly a short-lived gym and before that, a thousand other doomed ventures, was wedged between a gas station turned car detailer and a Subway restaurant. The outside of the building was still painted with a few poorly sketched figures—a Speedoed man of obscene proportions, a girl in a karate suit with teeth like a monster's. The paint peeled and flaked into a sad confetti, and one day, when Cathy and Jill were eating at Subway, Jill noticed that one of the karate girl's feet was unfinished. Time, it seemed, had run out.

Ralph, a failed farmer looking to cut every corner, wouldn't even consider repainting. He hung a homemade sign with his name stenciled on it and kept the floors concrete instead of putting in wood. Hitting hard, he said, just learned the kids to skate better.

It was the middle of the day. Kids were still at school, and the parking lot was nearly empty, but when Jill turned in, she spotted a skinny orange-haired girl out back, smoking by the trashcans. With the girl was some other boy that looked like the nephew only shorter, fatter. Even though it was sunny and almost hot, both of them wore black hooded sweatshirts.

Jill didn't bother parking. She pulled around the building as if she were going through a drive-thru. With the tires still rolling, she hit the button and the window went down. You Nicole? she hollered.

She expected to scare the girl. She wanted to. It'd be nice to see somebody else jump for a change, but instead, the girl turned slowly, and her mouth hung open just like the nephew's, and she closed and opened her eyes for such a duration that Jill felt the moment as if it were unfolding in a kind of slow-motion.

Nickie, the girl said, and then broke into a lethargic gurgle of thick laughter that made Jill wonder if the girl was about to vomit.

The boy standing beside her snorted. With some violence, he dragged the dirty sleeve of his sweatshirt under his nose. Then he looked back over his shoulder.

Nickie Dickey, the girl said.

Jill reached for the radio knob and twisted the volume down, but the radio wasn't on. I don't care what your friends call you.

Nickie's shoulders shook. She seemed to be trying to open her eyes. Then she stuck out her tongue and said, Blahhhh.

The boy hissed. He had a vicious rash around his mouth.

The engine idled and made a snapping noise.

Nickie blinked and stumbled toward the car. Hey, she said, as if it was the first time any of them were speaking, can you take us somewhere?

Around Nickie's neck was a black leather choker studded with a line of fake diamonds that caught the light. Seeing this, or perhaps something else, something familiar, Barbara smiled and, like Cathy had taught her, blew air through her lips. She wagged her little arms and beat her fists against the seat.

Yo, Nickie said. Whose baby is that?

As Nickie came forward, her sweatshirt fell open, and Jill saw the tight T-shirt riding up. Nickie was boney, but the skin around her belly was loose and white, like the hide around something dead.

That's my baby, Nickie said, and she was coming closer, but the toe of her boot hung in the gravel. She lurched and caught herself on the car door. That's my little Barbie. Before Jill could think better of it, her foot was punching the gas, and the car was jerking forward, and in the rearview mirror, she saw Nickie fall down. She was rolling around on the ground, and it was hard to tell if the girl was laughing or crying, but the claw of her hand was reaching after them.

Jill didn't look both ways before she hit the road. She didn't even stop. She popped the curb, and there was a terrible scraping sound, and they might have been killed, and in the back seat, Barbara just laughed and laughed.

≈

A truck came close, and the driver—a piggish man in a straw hat—made twisted faces at Jill and yelled at her. His window was up, and now Jill's was too, and the man didn't honk, but when his mouth opened, she saw the white of his tongue. It was a strangely silent assault, and afterward, the man hit the gas and pulled far in front of Jill. There was an EAT BEEF sticker plastered to his bumper.

Jill slowed the car down to a crawl. She didn't know where she was going anymore.

In the backseat, Barbara grinned and howled. Then she squeezed her eyes shut and giggled. She rubbed at her face with her fists, and by the time they'd turned onto South

Main, she was licking her lips and fighting to keep her eyes open.

Cathy said sometimes a nap was just what a baby needed to turn things around. Jill wondered what would do that for her, what would be the thing that made all the difference.

She couldn't give Barbara back to Nicole like she'd planned. The girl was just a baby herself, and that was the least of the problems. The nephew was certainly not an option, and his mother, Cathy's sister, was a real head case. Jill hadn't seen it for herself, but according to Cathy, who didn't like to talk about it much, the nephew never had a chance. His mother packed the house with all manner of things from newspapers to empty milk cartons to VHS tapes she said she felt bad for because nobody had any use for them anymore. Cathy said the house and everything in it was a real fire hazard, and she wouldn't be surprised if one day a call came in, and she'd have to go unearth her own sister's charred and unrecognizable body.

Sometimes Jill felt that way, like the world was closing in on her. There was a time when it seemed to Jill like she could go places, like she could be someone, but every day, this seemed less and less true. On the wheel, her hands were shaking worse than ever. That, the tremors, had started when her daddy started doing what he did, and when her mother started doing nothing except calling Jill a liar. But Jill didn't want to think about that. She didn't want to think or talk about it ever again. What she wanted was for things to be like they were without Barbara. What she wanted, she realized, just about the time the light by the Presbyterian Church turned, was a strong drink.

She'd have to make a U-turn and drive five or six miles in the other direction to get to Mike's. Foxy Lady was closer—was, in fact, almost already in sight.

Jill looked up at the mirror. Barbara was out now for sure. Her mouth was open, and a line of drool dripped on her shirt. Her arm hung down over the edge of the car seat, as if she'd dropped something important but tired herself out reaching for it.

Every summer, babies fried in cars, usually in the Walmart parking lot. But it wasn't that hot, Jill thought now as the wind came in the window. Just a little warm. Barbara would be okay. She'd be just fine. It would only be a minute or two. It'd be more likely for her to get kidnapped than to burn up. Jill laughed to herself. That'd be one way, she thought. But she didn't really believe in kidnappers, not in Black Creek anyway.

Jill pulled off the road, and when the car stopped, she half-expected Barbara to wake up, but Barbara didn't. She kept right on sleeping even when Jill rolled down the rest of the windows and cut the engine and got out of the car and shut the door. She slept through it all like some kind of princess who, one day, will wake up and see that everything has changed.

Jill took one last look, and then she headed on inside.

The Foxy Lady was Black Creek's only strip club and calling it a club was a bit of a stretch. It was really just an old house with a few walls knocked out and a bar in the living room. The floor was still carpeted, and you had to pass through the kitchen—which was grimy but still furnished with all the appliances—to get to the bathroom, and if you sat on the toilet, you stared into the tub, and if you stood over the toilet, you could read a framed copy of the Christian poem "Footprints."

The owner and sole proprietor of The Foxy Lady had inherited the property from his mother, and there were things he'd changed and things he hadn't. The tub, after all, sometimes came in handy. Everyone, even the cops, seemed to know that The Foxy Lady offered a wide range of services.

One of Jill's exes—not the construction guy or the porno watcher but one prior—had been a regular, and when Jill and Cathy first got together, Jill made Cathy take her. Cathy didn't like going to Foxy Lady much, but Jill got a real kick out of it, doing what her ex had done. She experimented with wearing flannel shirts and large gold belt buckles. She smashed her fist against things—the wall mostly, just for the hell of it. She even ordered the drink he liked to drink, rum and coke.

Just now, though, she asked the bearded bartender for vodka with anything, and anything turned out to be Tang, which was just fine. Jill sat at the bar and drank it down and asked for another. While the bartender poured, Jill said, You know anybody wanting a baby?

A what? the bartender said.

A baby.

He made a face like he'd smelled something bad, and Jill said, Never mind. She told him she was just kidding. It was a joke. Then she laughed in a way that wasn't so different from the sounds Cathy made when she was playing with Barbara. Ha-HA, ha-HA, ha-HA!

Why couldn't she be funny? Maybe if she could tell a good joke the world would turn right again. Being funny might make all the difference. There wasn't anybody else there, at least in the front part of the house, but Jill thought she heard something. She looked over her shoulder, toward the screen door, but it was coming from the back of the house, where the bedrooms were.

When she turned back, the bartender was eyeing her. He set the second drink down. Then he pressed the button on a stereo, and there was music.

Jill took her drink and went over to the couch that was printed with scenes from the English countryside. She sipped, and on the arm, she traced the outline of the woman's big blue skirt, the lacy trim of her bonnet. Her mama used to say things were better when ladies stayed at home and men were soldiers. People still had their values, her mama said. Jill was tracing the edge of the bonnet and getting to the round cheek when a girl in a neon green bikini came through a curtain beaded to look like the Mona Lisa.

Hola, the girl said.

She wasn't Spanish. Or Mexican. Nothing about her, Jill thought, could be more white, more pale. Her long flat belly. Her crimped hair. Even her eyelashes, Jill saw when the girl sat down beside her, were white.

Bet you burn, Jill said. The drink was leaving a film in her mouth.

The girl stared. Her eyes were a dull blue.

In the sun, Jill said. When it's hot.

Oh, the girl said. She sat back from Jill and dusted something like crumbs off her chest. Yeah, Mama always made me wear Coppertone.

Jill nodded and took a drink. It was strong, and it was helping. The edges of the room spun a little. That's good, she said.

The girl sighed.

No, Jill said, as if the girl was arguing with her. It's good that your mama cared like that.

The girl ran a thumb under the waistband of the bikini. There was a red mark where the elastic cut at her skin. She wanted me to be in the movies, the girl said.

Jill snorted. My mama just wanted me to go away.

The girl laughed without smiling, and the bartender coughed, cleared his throat.

Jill held the drink. The Tang wasn't the best. She thought she might throw up soon. She considered going to the bathroom. She could hang her head over the bowl. She could read the "Footprints" poem. She knew it was about Jesus, about never being alone. Instead, she kept talking.

They can really mess you up if you stop to think about it. Mamas, I mean. And Daddies too. Daddies especially. When they want to.

Jill's thoughts were turned around backward. It seemed like she was getting to the right place but in a stuttering way that could make a person crazy. She felt something fluttering at her temple and flinched before she realized it was the girl, brushing the hair out of Jill's eyes. She'd scooted closer and looked hurt, maybe even a little angry when Jill shrank from her. What little eyebrows she had were knitted up, wrinkling her forehead. She was never pretty enough for the movies. That was plain to see. You do like girls, she said, right?

The bearded bartender was watching them. It seemed like the same song was playing over and over again, some generic R&B. Just then, Jill could have sworn it was getting a little louder.

Why else would you come? the girl said.

Now, Jill thought. Now she would go to the bathroom. She tried to get up, but before she could, something was pressing her back against the scenes of the English countryside, against another time, another place.

I know what you need, the girl said, and if before she'd seemed like a sullen teenager hell-bent on getting a sunburn, now, in an instant, she'd become an all-knowing epitome of at least one kind of experience. She was like a ballerina, performing a show she'd rehearsed for years. She pivoted off and away from the couch and shimmied down to a squat, and then she was spreading Jill's knees as far apart as her own.

Jill needed to pee. She meant to tell the girl so when she heard a noise, she said, Did you hear that?

The girl grinned as she plastered her thin lips against Jill's knee.

Jill cocked her head. It was the sound of a rusted hinge that might have been a truck dropping a ramp at the convenience store across the street. Or it could have been closer, in the parking lot, a door opening or closing.

Can you turn that down? Jill said to the bartender. The music.

She made a move to push the girl away, but the girl was stronger than she looked. A vein pulsed in her shoulder as she gripped Jill's calves, and for a minute, she *was* like a girl in a movie. Something in the girl's face. She was dangling off the edge of a building, hanging on for dear life. Please, that girl would say. Help me.

The music was even louder now, at least that's how it sounded in Jill's head. She looked down at the girl who was, just then, licking Jill's shin bone. She looked so young, like a kid with a popsicle.

That. There was another sound, clear and distinct and definitely Barbara. With more resolve, more confidence than Jill had felt in years, she shoved, and the girl lost her balance and fell over backward. Dimly, Jill saw the girl's face, more surprised than angry as she fell. She was someone's baby, losing her footing. She was falling through the air, plummeting to a gruesome death.

From some distance, it seemed, Jill heard the bartender calling after her *hey, bills to pay, what the fuck*. But she was already through the door and out in the lot. The door of the car was open, and she ran to it, unaware of her own voice, the rising chant. No, no, no, no, no . . .

Barbara's bags were still there. The clothes and toys and bottles and other junk Jill had packed that morning. I'll take her back, she'd decided. I'll take her back where she belongs. She'd been certain it was the right thing to do. She shouldn't be responsible for a baby, for a life. She didn't feel like she could be responsible for anything.

And now Barbara was gone. The car seat was empty, and Jill half-drunk and out of her mind with terror, lifted the bags and the floor mats, and looked under the seats as if Barbara might be playing some trick, as if she were old enough to consider the ways she might fool a person.

Jill even thought she heard Barbara laughing. Then she knew she heard it, and raising her head from the floorboard to look out the windshield, she saw the muscled back of a woman wearing high heels and a pink sparkly one-piece, and when this woman turned around, Jill saw that she was holding Barbara.

Jill rose up so quickly she slammed her head against the top of the car, but she kept moving. She ran, tripping over a rock, turning her ankle but lurching forward, and from a certain perspective, she and Nicole didn't look so different, stumbling ahead, reaching for something to catch themselves. All of those kids skating in circles at Ralphie's Roller Rama, breaking their arms and legs. Kids, well, people were so delicate when you got down to it. There was hardly anything so fragile.

The stripper must have thought so, because when Jill reached for the baby, the woman hesitated only for a few seconds, and then seeing, recognizing something in Jill's face, she handed Barbara over.

Jill closed her eyes and pressed Barbara to her chest. Oh my God, she said and said again. There you are. Here I am. Jesus.

The stripper watched. She was much older than the blonde girl, much older than Jill, too, and she was tall. She looked down her nose. You shouldn't leave a baby in a car like that.

Jill stammered something about thinking it would be okay, just for a minute, such a nice day.

It don't matter! the woman said. It don't matter what kind of day it is. You don't leave a baby ever.

Jill's whole body was bobbing up and down in an exaggerated show of agreement.

A baby can die, the woman said.

I don't know, Jill said.

The woman rolled her eyes and adjusted herself. She popped the strap of her bathing suit, shifting from one heel to the other. People take babies for granted, she said. People would pay a lot of money for a pretty baby like that.

I don't know, Jill said again. It seemed like all there was to say. I don't know what I'm doing.

She meant she didn't know what she was doing with Barbara. She didn't know what she was doing at the Foxy Lady or with Cathy, and she didn't know about a lot of things which were larger and not yet formed in her mind.

Jill patted Barbara's back. She studied the woman, and the woman looked back at her until Jill finally understood. She shifted Barbara to her shoulder and reached in her pocket. She pulled out a wadded five and a couple of ones. She handed them over, and the woman took them. She was smiling now, and in a sweet slow drawl, she said, Pleasure.

Jill said yeah.

The stripper blew a kiss at Barbara. Y'all take care now.

≈

They were home a few hours before Cathy got back, and in that time, Jill did things she'd never done by herself before. Cathy usually stepped in. Cathy usually took over. But now it was just Jill, giving Barbara a bath in the kitchen sink. She bumped Barbara's head on the faucet and put her pajama pants on backwards, but they figured it out. Eventually, they got it right.

Jill fed Barbara a bottle, burped her, changed her, and then laid her down in the crib upstairs. She found a book and read from it. The story was meant for a much older kid, but Jill kept reading. After a while, she eased up from the chair, turned off the lights, and watched Barbara for a few more minutes before she made her way down the hall and the stairs.

Jill didn't feel like a mother. She didn't feel like she was entirely herself, either. There was always some distance, some spiritual gap she couldn't seem to bridge. But maybe that was normal. Maybe that's how everyone felt.

I'm so sexy? she said like a question. She went over to Porky's cage. He was holding tight to his perch, looking at himself in the mirror. Jill watched him through the metal bars. Porky was only a year old. He could live ninety-nine more. He would outlive all of them. Cathy kept saying how they needed to make up a will, for Porky, and now for Barbara.

It hurts, Porky answered. Whatchya think? It hurts.

Jill stared at him a little longer. Then she threw the sheet over the cage.

She was sprawled in the chair with the television on by the time Cathy finally came home.

Howdy, Cathy said, when she opened the door and closed it behind her. She stepped out of her boots and set her duffel by the door. She unclipped the talkie and switched it off. She stopped and listened, then pointed up. She asleep?

Jill nodded.

You did that? Cathy said.

Jill shrugged.

Wow, Cathy said. She took a deep breath and let it out again. She made her way to the matching chair and fell back in it. She stared at the TV, and by the look on her face, Jill could tell that the wreck had been bad, that probably someone was dead.

They both stared at the television. It was a nature show, something about the way plants are adapting to conditions of global warming. The screen showed a time-lapsed video of a desert plant, its leaves widening to catch more of the morning's dew.

I took Barbara for a drive, Jill said.

Did it work? Cathy said.

I guess so.

Good, Cathy said. Then she turned and looked at Jill. Show me your hands, she said like she did every day. She'd been after Jill to go see a doctor about the tremors. She warned that it might be a sign of a medical condition. Maybe something serious.

Jill rolled her eyes, but she stuck out her hands. They still shook but maybe less so. Five fingers were painted and five still weren't.

Here, Cathy said. The bottle of Blue Blazes was on the table. Cathy turned on the lamp and went to unscrew the lid, but Jill took it from her. You, she said. She motioned for Cathy to put her hands on the table.

Cathy rolled her tongue and shook her head. Nails, that's something I don't do.

Jill, though, wouldn't take no for an answer. She thought of the girl at Foxy Lady. I know what you need, she said with surprising force.

Cathy watched with eyes that were tired but searching, and when she looked at Jill like that, Jill got the feeling that Cathy saw things deep inside her, as if in Jill, there was still so much to be found.

Jill shoved a clear spot on the table between them. She tapped the varnished wood until finally, Cathy relented. Finally, Cathy spread her fingers out flat.

Jill took the cap off the bottle. I think we should teach Porky something new.

Cathy frowned. Like what?

Jill shrugged. I don't know. Maybe some of those codes you use.

Cathy laughed. Code 33, 999.

See? Jill said. It'd be funny. Porky the paramedic parrot. After a while, she added, I could learn too.

Jill held onto Cathy's hand to steady her own. The lines weren't perfect, but she kept painting. Even when it was uncomfortable to lean like that, even when she felt a muscle cramp, she would keep on until she couldn't, reaching out across the little table and the remote control and whatever else that was piled there between them.

OF WOLVES

The gall bladder, Candy said, is left of the pancreas.

Gall bladder, pancreas. Gall bladder, pancreas. The pancreas was right, so the gall bladder left, Candy said and said again. She saw the body parts with faces and legs and arms and hands that the gall bladder, angry as he was, balled into fists and shook at the pancreas. I've had it up to here with you!

Mnemonic devices. Mind cartoons. This was what Candy had been reduced to. She gritted her teeth until they squeaked. She used to memorize things—license plates, for instance—without even trying. See it to know it, her father had said. That's my Candy.

But she wasn't his Candy anymore. She was forty now, and nothing came easy.

The frog in the tray was starting to smell. Candy gripped the tweezers, but her hand shook. She pushed up the sleeve of her robe and grabbed her own wrist, dug her thumb into the meat between the thin bones until her fingers went numb.

Gall bladder, pancreas. Pancreas says, *I'm outta here! I'm through with you! Sayonara, gall!*

Just slow down, Marty said. He was mumbling, but Candy could understand. Tell me what happened.

Marty was still in bed. He was still in his boxer shorts. He was still asleep.

Candy, at her vanity, dug at the frog. Gall bladder says, Beat it then! See if I care!

She glanced up at the mirror, but Marty's eyes were closed. His mouth was smashed open against the pillow, so that his tongue showed pink and wet.

Candy went back to the frog. Adios, muchacho!

There was a time when Candy's mother Sue had tried to explain her daughter, mostly to teachers who were, they said, simply voicing their concerns. Candy tries too hard sometimes, Sue would say. That's her problem. She just wants everything to be perfect.

In many ways, Sue didn't understand her daughter, but she'd gotten this part right. What she'd said was as true then as it was now. Candy had a desperate need to make sense of the world. She wanted things to line up in some order of importance, and when they didn't, she'd do the rearranging until she could discern some reasonable relationship between cause and effect. Candy would be the one to make sense of it all.

Sometimes this sense was as small as the insertion of a period rather than a comma. The reporter who worked under Candy, The Airhead, could never correct her own splices no matter how many times Candy pointed them out.

Other times, Candy constructed what she believed to be the larger order of things—the fact that it was her mother's penchant for clutter and spontaneity and what she called "life" that made Candy the way she was, what some, including those concerned teachers, had called obsessive. Neurotic. Controlling. These words were better than those that passed between Candy's classmates. They couldn't come up with anything better than weird or weirdo.

Logic of a certain kind and magnitude—what made a person a person, for instance—was not what one would call pleasant, but Candy felt a certain satisfaction in her own knowledge, a haughtiness about the things she knew and assumed others didn't.

It was pitiful, Candy thought, the way people went on about things, like they had no will or say, like they were sacks of bodies without bones and brains. Candy, for example, was simply explaining that a comma was needed every time you used a conjunction to join two independent clauses when The Airhead ran out of the office with her face caved in on itself and her nose full of snot.

This is why, Candy told Marty, The Airhead is on a fast track to nowhere. In every instance, Candy preferred knowledge to ignorance. Her teachers had appreciated what they called her curiosity and her knack for proper sentence construction even if Candy was a bit ruthless when it came to literature, to understanding a character's actions and motivations. She was one of those students that came to a story or a novel from a place of righteous expectation. In "My Papa's Waltz," she could not get over the fact that the father had a drinking problem. Who cared about this rare moment of tenderness between child and parent? And who could take seriously the blind man in "Cathedral"? They were all just a bunch of drug addicts after all. Regular hedonists with no control. Forgiveness, to Candy, meant nothing, and it seemed, said the teacher, that empathy meant even less.

Candy's essays and presentations were tiresome, but she never missed a deadline or forgot to introduce quoted material without a proper signal phrase. Such details, her teachers agreed, were important and in fact, essential to success. These fundamental concepts composed the very foundations of good writing, and anything Candy lacked was too difficult to identify, too complicated to correct in the proofreader's shorthand teachers favored when they were staring down the barrel of a hundred freshman essays. A, their tired hands scrawled, and it was Candy's own heavy-browed glare, a look so volatile as to foster its own apparition, that came so easily to mind even when the teachers were in their socks in their own homes with their coffee and their cats, and so, seeing this child's face as if it were there and full of terror in the very room with them, they scratched out the minus. What did, they thought, a few points matter? What did any of it matter when you got down to it?

And this was just the sort of existential thinking that would have driven Candy into a lip-splitting, eye-blackening rage. After a few exemplary incidents, those kids that called her a weirdo weren't brave enough to say it to her face. They'd seen what could happen. They'd seen what Candy could do.

But in the classroom, Candy's rigor and dedication as well as her work for the student newspaper—who could forget that stellar article on why they were the Fighting Falcons?—pushed Candy's teachers to suggest journalism, and, as she had always done, Candy followed their instructions to the soulless letter. There was about her the nature of a robot, as if under that skull of matted brow and hair there was not a mind but instead a set of wires and chips.

All of that had been so long ago, but school, specifically grades 1–12, was somehow still the defining experience of Candy's existence. Except for the four years she'd spent at Clemson, Candy had lived her whole life in Black Creek in the same house as her mother.

Sympathetic people said it wasn't that Candy was an unfeeling person. It wasn't, as one especially bored teacher had hoped, that Candy was a sociopath. It was just, these poor sensitive souls said, that parts of Candy had been arrested. She hadn't developed in all the ways a girl should, and, too, her curiosity—which was actually more like an aggressive interrogation—was manifested in the very shapes and lines of her physical appearance. There was the squirreled brow she refused to pluck or even, as Sue gently suggested, shape, and this brow, bully that it was, dwarfed and shaded every other feature of Candy's face that might have held or expressed joy, passion, or even a real sense of sadness. And, in a part of the country that favored monograms and pearls and, on occasion, full skirts and hose, Candy wore baggy slacks that hung loose in the seat and rode tight in the waist and the ankles which gave way to a pair of odorous orthopedic sandals.

What would Candy do, they all wondered, when her mother passed away?

There was, in the house, a general wafting of death and decay that came, yes, from the sandals and the calloused feet that wore them, but also this smell, this horrible sweetness was on account of the small animals that Candy had recently began dissecting.

Sue, a woman with plenty of her own predilections, was terrified of global warming and, consequently, any aerosols including the only air fresheners that had any effect. So it was with a kind of pleading sense of defeat, just the sort of attitude Candy despised, that Sue lit bundle after bundle of herbs and also long sticks of flea market patchouli that smelled more than anything like the barbecue Black Creek was supposedly known for, but the incense did nothing about the odor of decomposition except perhaps make the smell of dead animals a degree more appetizing.

Please, Sue begged, but she didn't bother asking Candy to stop anything that she was doing. After forty years together, Sue knew better. She did ask if Candy the sweetheart, Candy her little dove, could perhaps consider the outdoors a better place for her projects? Say, for instance, the shed?

But the light in the shed, where Candy's father had spent most of his time when he was alive—hiding, Sue said—was just a dusty old bulb and no comparison to Candy's high wattage vanity lamp, and anyway, if the animals stunk to Sue in a way they most certainly did not to Candy, good enough! In the first place, it was Sue's fault that Candy had never learned the workings of a frog's intestines or, for another example, the unique respiratory system of a worm. When they'd got to this unit in school, Sue had banned Candy from participating. She'd gone so far as to organize a protest, a picket line against animal cruelty. But such causes found little support in South Carolina, and though a few whimpering mothers had brought protest sandwiches and protest coffee—they felt for Sue, they really did—after an hour or so, it was only Candy and Sue, Candy sitting on the curb with her chin in her hand, watching her mother, who, for the occasion, had drawn whiskers across her cheeks and an upside-down heart for a nose— hold up a poster until her arms shook, screaming, No slice! No mice! No slice! No mice!

Candy tried to explain that the classes didn't even use mice. There was a worm, and then a cow's eye, and then a fetal pig, and finally, the culmination of it all and the basis for the final exam—a shark. But Sue wasn't listening to Candy. Or perhaps she didn't care. It's the principle of the matter, Sue said, and though she was beautiful and Candy was most certainly not, there was something in common about their persons even if they couldn't see it.

They might have, in their shared adulthood, become something like friends as many mothers and daughters will, but instead, they simply continued much as they had before, and at forty, Candy spent most of her time alone, reading a biology textbook she'd found at the Friends of the Library semiannual sale. She was using this book as a guide to learning the workings of small animals, vertebrate and invertebrate. It was slow-going, and though she'd never admit it, new concepts didn't come as easily for Candy as they once had, but she still had the same determination, the same drive to, as the Fighting Falcons motto said, Believe and achieve!

To Sue, Candy said, You can't tell me what to do.

A lot of people, besides Candy's teachers, thought Candy had a few problems. Black Creek was a small town where, everyone conceded, not much happened. It was probably tough for Candy to figure out how, every week, she and the splice-happy reporter would figure out how to fill all ten pages of the newspaper. It was no wonder that every now and then, there'd be some article the drugstore coffee-drinkers would describe as "off the wall." An editorial, for example, about data collection and the ways in which the government would use the records of your Piggly Wiggly purchases as evidence against you in the case for terrorism. And what about that other column Candy wrote about the dangers of marijuana addiction? Sure, dope was bad, and some of it, that stuff they made with household cleaners, for example, was real bad—everybody could agree on that, but the ferocity of Candy's conviction, the sharpness of her tone (These people are the very dredges, the open sewage of our modern society.) made you feel downright sorry for the druggies. Addiction, the pharmacist said, was an illness, after all.

In this way, Candy was deft at achieving but often with the opposite of her intended effect.

Most everybody figured Candy was just doing her best to make a name for herself, to break out as young people were always wanting to do. Black Creek was a conservative place, but the people were surprisingly sympathetic. They forgave one another, or at least pretended to, and maybe this was why, after Clemson, Candy had come back. Even if, despite all those research-heavy articles on the school's mascot, she hadn't been made teenage queen of the Black Creek universe (weirdo!). Even if she didn't get along so well with her mother. Even if this and a million other things stood as good reasons for Candy to make a life elsewhere, maybe being away at Clemson had taught her that she wouldn't be accepted—not even a little bit—anywhere but here.

Candy didn't talk much about college, and in a way, it was like that time in Candy's life wasn't quite real, as if she could only exist in one place in her own particular and puzzling way.

Sue figured that, at the very least, Candy was a homosexual, and Sue, being the caftan-wearing, patchouli-burning free spirit that she had carefully crafted herself into being, spent a lot of time reassuring Candy that she wouldn't have a problem, she wouldn't say a word if Candy wanted to, someday, say, bring over another little dove.

Candy didn't answer one way or another except to say, Gawd! in such a way that made her seem somewhere near a quarter of her age, which was probably accurate in emotion if not intellect.

Sue remained convinced that homosexuality wasn't just one of Candy's problems but was, of course, the very crux of all of Candy's less than desirable traits—her irritations and her tantrums, what Sue referred to as "mood storms." Sue had a lot of interesting phrases. All would be revealed when Candy acknowledged her primal self as Sue had done during the post-intermission session of a Pink Floyd tribute concert.

With all this thought about cores of the self and girlfriends, Sue could not have been more shocked—and, admittedly, relieved—to hear, one morning, the deep notes of a man's voice coming from behind Candy's closed door. Sue's authentic primal self was actually far more conservative than she'd like to admit. So happy was Sue that she fell back in bed and back to sleep as if Candy's newfound and surprisingly conventional love life was a kind of lullaby, a bedtime story that, like Candy, had been constructed for the sole purpose of relaxing and comforting Sue herself.

Little did Sue know, about this or, according to Candy, anything else. This was not the first time Candy had been with Officer Marty. The first time had taken place in Candy's office, after hours, after The Airhead had left with a stack of grammar handbooks Candy had loaned her with relevant lessons flagged by yellow sticky notes. Yes, the first time with Marty was in the office of *The Record*, and some—those with a limited understanding of Candy-like individuals—would be surprised to know that Candy had been the initiator, that she'd been the one to grab Officer Marty by his meaty shoulders and pin him down across her desk, her face sweating and flashing nothing but irritation when Marty's hand inadvertently sent her cup of red pencils tumbling to the carpet.

Those first few kids who'd said, Weirdo—they would understand. They wouldn't have a problem imagining the action Candy could take.

And maybe little did Sue know, but little would she have been surprised if made privy to these juicy details because her daughter might have been anti-social and a bit, you might say, of a loner, but Candy was never timid, and, in fact, once, when Sue had come at her with a leather-bound grooming kit, Candy had wrestled Sue to the ground and grabbed the tweezers and swore she'd shove a hole right through Sue's eye.

She hadn't gone that far, but still, Sue understood that within Candy rested a power made dark by the world and the people in it which Candy found to be a constant source of disappointment and frustration, boneless saps that they were.

Candy had those red pencils collected and back where they belonged, point down in the cup, before good old Officer Marty could zip his fly. My lands, Marty said, you're something.

And Candy, who by that time, was back in her office chair, told Officer Marty that if he ever had any hopes of becoming sergeant, he should really make an effort to be more specific when communicating. Saying a person is something, she said, is as good as saying a person is nothing.

She stared at Marty. Is that what you mean?

And good old Officer Marty, poor soul, said exactly what he meant, which wasn't much. I don't know, he said, and it was then that one of those red pencils, sharpened to a fine point, flew like a dart beside the red gristle of Marty's ear.

Candy was tough. That much was certain. And not in the moments leading up to that time or the weeks after did she ever believe she thought (and she certainly didn't feel) anything remotely lovey-dovey (one of Sue's favorite phrases) about Officer Marty. He was neither handsome nor charming with his hard, low paunch and his skinny legs and his typical tearful story—so trite, Candy could have finished his sentences—of his recent separation from his wife Deborah and what he feared would soon become a custody battle because what Candy didn't know was that good old Officer Marty had a taste for some of the things he found in the pockets and the trunks of Black Creek's less desirables. My boy, Marty said when he got talking about his son. My baby boy, Marty nearly moaned, and it was all Candy could do not to slap him.

But there was something about Marty—the way he let Candy grab him by the shoulders and throw him down, for example, or the way he smiled when she threw the pencil—that Candy found attractive, that Candy found downright irresistible. If anyone had asked her about Marty, which absolutely no one did, Candy would have said that Officer Marty, like The Airhead and like Sue, could stand to learn a thing or two including but not limited to the importance of specific language and the proper identification of a frog's pancreas which was to the right of the gall bladder.

That morning, which really was the fourth time they'd been together, Candy was working at the frog with the heavy biology book splayed out across the vanity. She was, in fact, using the very same tweezers that she'd promised to send through to the nut she said Sue had for a brain. See there, Candy said. There is the small intestine.

Candy spoke, like always, with authority, but the truth was she wasn't sure. She wasn't sure where the stomach ended and the small intestine began. The picture in the book didn't look like real life, and anyway, Candy was hav-ing a hard time concentrating.

Behind her, Marty was waking up.

Something about this, their fourth time together, had been different, and even though Candy kept picking at the frog that she'd trapped in the tangled coil of the water hose and then suffocated in a Mason jar, she was, in her mind, making a list of things that weren't the same.

Officer Marty, number one, had rolled Candy over—rather clumsily but ultimately successfully and with some force—so that he was on top. This was a definite difference.

Difference number two, they'd been in an actual bed instead of across her desk or in the back of his patrol car.

Number three, Officer Marty had either lost weight or put on some muscle in his thighs. He had a more balanced feel to him, and Candy kept glancing up from the dead frog to the reflection of Officer Marty in her vanity mirror.

He was awake now. He'd pushed on his glasses, and he was looking at his phone, and before Candy could catch herself, she said, Is it her?

Marty blinked, which for him, sometimes seemed more like a twitch, a kind of compulsive squinting that, like his pathetic "my boy" refrain, bothered Candy immensely. Is it who?

Deborah, Candy said. On the phone?

Marty looked back at the phone like he needed Candy to tell him what it was he held and what he was supposed to do with it. His chin tripled when he tucked it so, and Can-dy scratched the part about him dropping a few pounds. When he shook his head, the chins quivered. It's about a girl, he said. They found one. Down in the creek. Dead.

Candy watched him in the mirror, and for a minute, neither one of them moved. They might have been two figures in a bizarre portrait, shirtless fat Marty in bed with his phone and Candy with her splayed frog and still in her bath robe. It would have been just the sort of art, full of reflection and symbol and secret emotion, that Candy would have hated no matter how hard her teachers would have tried to get her to see what it was that brought these two together or, conversely, what kept them apart and what ultimately their experience said about the rest of us.

She's got, the teachers had often said about Candy, so much potential.

Then Candy moved. Candy whirled around on the silly backless vanity stool and said, What girl? You didn't tell me about any girl.

Marty's whole body was squinched down on itself—his eyes, his neck, his shoulders. Some people don't like talking about work.

Some people aren't me.

Marty looked at her. He took a breath and let it out his nose, which rattled. Then he pushed off the covers, swung his legs over the side of the bed, and reached for his pants.

They found her in the creek, Marty said.

You said that.

She was dead.

You said that, too.

So I did tell you, Marty said. He stood up, zipped his pants, buckled his belt. Even if he had lost some weight, he was still fat. Or at least he looked fat from where Candy was on the stool.

We're still trying to find the parents, Marty said. It's hush-hush.

People have a right to know, Candy said.

Marty opened his mouth, and even though he was awake, he looked as slack as when he'd been sleeping with his face jammed against the pillow. He buttoned the last button on his shirt. Then he reached back to his pocket, and for a single absurd second, Candy thought he would take out his wallet. That he would take out his wallet and reach inside and give her money. It was a ridiculous thought. No sense to it. Marty was only checking to make sure he had everything, and when he saw that he did, he kissed Candy on the top of the head. He told her he'd see her soon.

What's the girl's name? Candy said, but Marty was gone.

Alone, Candy sat with her jaw hanging loose, a look she found maddening when she caught it in other people. In the window, a fly buzzed, drawn by the smell of the frog.

Candy had sensed a difference in Marty, and now she thought maybe the dead girl was it. Black Creek was a small town, the kind of town, Marty would say later, where kids didn't die. Outside of the small-time drug busts, Marty's job primarily consisted of speeding tickets and cat rescues. A dead girl in the creek wouldn't be anything Marty was used to seeing, and it wasn't the kind of thing Candy was used to writing about, but to Candy, every story was the same and constructed from a kind of formula. She'd put all the pieces together—the hook, the news, the backstory, and the future cast.

In the window, the fly buzzed, and Candy spun back around, and it was then that she'd realized that her robe had fallen open, that when she'd turned back toward Marty, not as a lover to a lover but as an editor to a cop, one of her breasts was bared.

The exposure was worse for being incomplete. If Candy had been without the robe at all, she might have said the revelation was of her own accord. But as it was, this small and loose sack, this evidence of human corporality, the inadvertent exposure of this breast let flow a rush of embarrassment and shame that, in Candy, quickly turned to anger and sometimes violence. When she stood up, the stupid stool crashed to the floor where Candy left it in her rush to reach for an old issue of *The Record*, which she took in her hand and made into a tube and thwacked so hard against the window that the glass, or something, cracked, and still, as Sue called out, as Sue yelled, Okay in there? the fly circled above Candy's head looking for a place to land.

The girl's name was Makeisha Toffer Powell. Candy managed to pull this information from a reluctant and surprisingly terse Officer Marty in addition to the following facts, which she wrote down in all caps in every other line of her reporter's notebook: 15 YRS OLD, DROWNING (ACCID? SUI? MURD?), 127 QUINBY PLACE.

This last part, which meant that Candy and Makeisha were practically neighbors, came as a bit of a shock. Candy tried to think of girls she'd seen around the neighborhood, but she couldn't remember anything specific. She'd never had much use for girls and after a certain age, didn't really think of herself as one. In her mind, they were all different versions of Sue, bouncing figures with little else to consider but boys and brows and perfumes.

There were always girls roaming the streets, prowling the sidewalks like they were looking for something to eat or otherwise get into. But to Candy, they were all the same. She couldn't tell one from the next.

That's the grandmother's house, Marty said about the place on Quinby and then he told her to go on, to get out of the office. He was going to lose his job, his pension if Candy didn't watch out.

They were sitting at his desk, which was different than Candy's desk in that it was out in the open of a large room full of other desks, a positioning that prohibited Candy from certain courses of action. Even in December, the place was hot with bodies and computers. Nobody was watching them, but Marty kept looking over his shoulder.

It's your own shadow, Candy said, but she got up. She pulled her sweater out and over her chest. Are we on?

Marty pushed at his glasses. His eye twitched, and his head swiveled on his neck. I don't know. I might have Roger.

Roger. The boy. My boy, as Marty would say if he were spinning his sad little tale.

You've gotta eat.

I don't think so.

Fine.

Hey.

Candy was walking away from him now. She kept on like she didn't hear.

Wait, Marty said. Stop.

Candy stopped. She'd eaten too much for breakfast. Sue's strange curried eggs had turned to a hard knot in her belly. This was what she told herself. This was what she tried to believe as Marty motioned for her to come back, and as she did, after only a few seconds, exactly what she was told.

Marty was writing something down on a sticky pad. His handwriting was terrible, partly because, Candy saw, he held his pen all wrong. She was about to tell him so when he tore off the sheet and handed it to her.

Candy held the paper far away. Then she brought it up to her face until she could make out that it said, Twilight.

Maybe tomorrow, Marty said.

There was real regret in his voice, like he was sorry to say it, like he was saying he was sorry.

Candy looked at him, the wobbly neck, the twitching face, the lips he licked to obsession. If asked, she would have said that Officer Marty was a pathetic, repulsive little man.

Corina's, she said. Tomorrow.

≈

All that afternoon, they'd worked on proofing an issue, which had taken hours longer than it should have on the sole account, according to Candy, of The Airhead's willful ineptitude. Apparently, the reporter, who was actually just an unpaid intern from the technical college and for whom the job was intended by the school to be an exciting and beneficial learning experience, had not taken full advantage of the grammar handbooks Candy had so graciously lent, and when Candy asked why she hadn't completed the night's homework, the intern said, of all things, that she'd had a date, that her boyfriend had (Can you believe it?!) asked her to marry him.

The copy teemed with splices as well as fragments and capitalization errors. Sentences bled together down the page.

The Airhead had forgotten herself. That is, she'd forgotten who she was speaking to, and while Candy marked and slashed with the red pencil, The Airhead went on about how the boyfriend (now—imagine!—she could call him a fiancé) had ordered their favorite type of pizza and how he'd wiped cheese off her chin just before he'd gotten down on one knee and thank goodness because the waiter took their picture, and the whole restaurant clapped . . .

And it wasn't that Candy was ignoring her. In fact, Candy found it hard to ignore anything, and so could not typically and efficiently do more than one task at a time, and just now, after five, she was losing ground on the proofing and giving in to the scene The Airhead was bent on creating, except for the man on one knee in Candy's mind had a triple chin and a twitching eye, and when The Airhead took a breath, Candy said, Get out!

And while The Airhead stood gaping with just that stupid expression, Candy said, Go! Out of here! Now!

She said some other things then, things that only The Airhead would remember later. It was a vile, vitriolic little stream that sent The Airhead scrambling around her desk, gathering up her tote bag and her water bottle, and the poor girl actually let out a little yelp when she finally closed the door behind her.

When she was gone, Candy stood in the middle of the empty office. Her feet were planted flat on the floor. Her hands were fists at her sides, and if she felt any regret, if she had the slightest sense of misplaced aggression, she pushed it out of mind, or, rather, she pushed it far down inside herself beside the knot Candy blamed on Sue. With a military flair, she spun on her heel and marched back to her desk where she continued to proof and correct in the old-fashioned paper-and-pencil way she preferred.

Candy took her temper from her father. This according to Sue. Candy's own memory of her father was specific but maddeningly minimal and consisted primarily of a sawdust smell and the soft knees of slacks worn thin.

Sue, though, remembered everything and liked most of all to regale Candy with stories about her father's own "mood storms."

He'd get mad at the least little thing, and he'd stomp around, and you could nearly see the smoke coming out of his nose, Sue said. It was best just to let him go out there to the shed and hide from life for a while. He'd be better the next day. You could just see all the bad stuff running out of him.

So Sue was right and she was wrong too because while Candy was prone to real and abiding anger, it seemed there was nothing she could do to release it. She wasn't better the next day. It seemed that all she did was get worse. Explosions such as what befell the unsuspecting, stupidly happy Airhead that afternoon were only illusions. Any eruption only fed a deeper well of malice that had been building practically since Candy was born.

She could feel the weight of it within her, this place where she pushed everything, and more so, she could feel the levity in others—in Sue worst of all but also in The Airhead and Marty and, Candy guessed, in Roger and Deborah, too. My boy, my boy! All of them acted and behaved with a kind of shallow irresponsibility to themselves and the world.

Under her desk, Candy struck at her stomach with a closed fist. The pancreas was right, so the gall bladder left. A comma here. No comma there.

≈

Corina's Mexican restaurant was in an older building downtown and all the buildings downtown, including the police station and the newspaper office, suffered from significant and occasionally terrifying bat infestations. Perhaps in an effort to cover the stink of guano and bats more generally, the owners and operators of Corina's mopped the floor a dozen or more times a day with quadruple the appropriate amount of Pine Sol. Still, the place smelled like a cave and the food carried interesting flavors of dirt and chemicals of the lemon-scented ammonia variety. Sue swore the food would kill people if the hole in the atmosphere didn't take care of everybody first.

Candy sat in a booth working on her second basket of tortilla chips. The chips made little cuts along her gums and under her tongue, and the salsa on these cuts was so painful as to be almost medicinal. Candy ate more. She ate faster.

She'd spent all of the previous day and, after the blow-up at The Airhead, half the night working at the proofs. Now the issue was at the printer, and so they were at work on the next edition, which would feature Candy's yet-to-be-written article about Makeisha Powell.

Candy had a start. That is, she had some facts. When they—the coroner with help from paramedics and Marty—pulled the body from the creek, they'd found, in the girl's pocket, a school ID with the Quinby Place address, and there, at 127, they'd found Makeisha's grandmother, bedridden, soiled, and nearly starved to death. At some point, maybe years ago, Mrs. Powell had suffered a stroke, and the best they could tell, Makeisha had been the one taking care of Mrs. Powell ever since. The parents, like a lot of parents in Black Creek, were nowhere anybody knew.

At Twilight Nursing Home, Mrs. Powell laid on her side and curled in on herself. Her hands were tucked to her chest, like a baby's, and she seemed not to notice that Candy was in the room.

Candy sat down in the chair and, after a minute, she pulled the chair closer. She stared at Mrs. Powell, and Mrs. Powell stared at a spot on the waxed tiled floor.

Candy took in air and let it out again. Then she reached into her purse and pulled out a copy of the photograph she'd found that morning in a school yearbook. There wasn't much to be told from it—just a girl with braids and a wide smile, and if you stared too long, as Candy had, the girl's face disintegrated into pixels, a kind of black and white confetti.

Still, Candy showed it to the woman, hoping it might have some effect.

She waited, but there was no response except the slow blink that Mrs. Powell kept up like a clock, like a part of herself that worked by mechanics and nothing else.

Your granddaughter, Candy said. Makeisha?

Another blink. Then nothing.

In the other room, some patients were watching *Young and the Restless*. Candy had seen the TV while she waited for the nurse at the front desk. Sue liked those shows, and it drove Candy crazy—the plotlines that went on for years, forever even, and just when you had it figured out, they threw in something else like a convict or a ghost that sent everything spinning in a new direction.

On the television, there was a sound like a gunshot, and as if it was fear that caused her to move, Candy reached out, grabbed Mrs. Powell's hand. The fingers were cool and hard as sticks, and Candy tried to make them hold onto the photograph.

Remember, she said, your granddaughter, Makeisha.

She studied the old woman's face, which was dull and void of expression, and still for a minute, a few seconds, Candy had a feeling that was equal parts plausible and unreasonable, that the woman was seeing her, that she was seeing the inside of her, and in the woman's yellow eyes, Candy saw Sue with a handful of fire and Office Marty on one knee and before him, she saw herself, and her belly was cut, and she was pointing to the way things were. She was saying, The gall bladder left! And, as clearly as if the old woman had a dissecting needle, Candy felt a sharp prick.

Without thought and without measure, Candy said, Please!

It was not a word she used often, and so, from her tongue, it carried a kind of trill, and in Mrs. Powell, there was a flicker, an undeniable shade of recognition, and Mrs. Powell did not take her eyes off Candy even when the nurse came in and said, Somebody should have told you. She's non-verbal.

The voice startled Candy.

She can't talk, the nurse said.

Because she's non-verbal, Candy said. She glared at the nurse, but the nurse didn't seem to notice.

I think she's still in there though, she said. I've worked here long enough to know it's possible. Anything is.

Candy turned back to Mrs. Powell. A line of spit ran down the woman's chin into a bubble that very prettily popped.

Now, at Corina's, Candy was waiting on Marty even if she was pretending otherwise. A part of her wanted to tell him about Mrs. Powell, but she wouldn't. Mrs. Powell she would add to the heap of things she did her best not to acknowledge, a regular stinking dump that would, too, house the vision with which Candy was just then confronted.

See it to know it. That's how Candy used to be and maybe in some ways, maybe in more ways than she thought, Candy hadn't changed all that much. To see Deborah was to know her, to see her hand in Marty's and Marty and The Boy, My Boy wearing their matching Fighting Falcon T-shirts. To see the family was to know the family and so much more, it was all Candy could do to shove her mouth full of enchiladas that tasted like dirt, like Earth, like the very world that caused Candy so much trouble and, if she were honest, pain, and she might have killed herself. She'd thought about it more than once. More than a lot of times. But if Marty was scared of his own shadow which was a shade composed not only of himself but of Deborah and My Boy and his pension and, of course, Candy, then Candy herself was terrified. It wasn't the doing—the slitting of the wrists or the tying of the noose—the procedure, that is, of suicide that scared her, but of that moment when she could do nothing else but accept what came as it came whether or not it conformed to her idea of structure. It was this very moment that, for Mrs. Powell, had expanded in such a way that it had become more than time, so that it was also a place, a dark pit without beginning or end or center from which a person could only languish and, if she was so lucky, scream.

So what Candy might have done was never what she did. What she did was stab at the greasy pool of rice and beans at the edge of the platter, and that night, when she came home growling and hitting at her stomach, Sue said, What did I tell you? It's all nothing but poison.

≈

Candy told Marty she was going to kill him. She told Marty, during the phone call she received late that night, that she planned to cut him up into little pieces and carry those pieces down to the alligators. She knew where there were some, a whole family, less than an hour away. And then, she would wrestle and kill the specific alligator, as Marty knew she was very capable of doing, and she would slice that alligator from Adam to anus and remove Marty's dismembered and now partially digested body to see which parts of him—the brain, she was betting—disappeared first.

This was what she told Marty. This was what she said.

On the other end of the line, Marty let loose a great hiccupping heave of a sob, and he said he was sorry, and he said Candy had every right to cut him up into little pieces and feed him to the family of alligators or whatever she wanted, and that in some ways, he felt like somebody had done the job already. It was the girl in the creek. Seeing her there in the water, pulling her out and holding her hand. That'd been his part, to hold her hand and pull, and it was almost like she would come alive, like in the fairy stories he read to his boy and that his own mother had read to him. Like the girl would open her eyes and ask for a prince or a father, for an answer of how long she'd been sleeping.

This stuff doesn't happen here, Marty said in between gulps for air. This isn't the kind of place where kids die.

Marty blew his nose, and when he was finished and another minute had passed, he said, Hello? Candy? Are you there?

Candy could hear him breathing through his mouth like he did when he was fast asleep, and in that space between them, in that relative silence, there was everything anyone wanted. There was in the calling out and the waiting a need so basic as to be shared by humans and animals alike, and as if in answer to some much larger question, Candy said, Yes. I'm still here.

Good, Marty said, and then he made a sound like a laugh but one in which there was no joy, only relief. That's good.

Because he was going to make some changes. He'd leave Deborah. He'd make sergeant. He'd take a couple of classes at Tech. I'll do, he said, whatever you want.

Candy was at her vanity. She'd had to throw the frog away. The smell had gotten too bad even for her, but the book was still there. The book was still open to the diagram, and now, as Marty rattled on about all his hopes and dreams, Candy traced with her finger the workings of the frog—the strange flag of the brain and the heart which seemed, in its central location, superior to a human's at least in terms of symmetry.

In the mirror, above the book, Candy saw herself. She knew what it was the old woman had seen, and she knew, too, what Mrs. Powell had asked of her as if the woman had opened her mouth and spoken more clearly than Marty was now.

Candy studied her reflection, her hair, her face, her neck. She loosened her robe, let it slip down over her broad shoulders. She put a hand over the place where her frog's heart would be, and she told Officer Marty exactly what she wanted.

≈

The house at 127 Quinby Place was empty. That isn't to say there wasn't furniture, but somehow, even with the coffee table and the sofa lounger and the chair with the doilies on the arms, the living room and every room thereafter gave the impression of things missing.

Hurry up, Marty said. He'd agreed to what she'd asked of him, but he didn't like it. I don't like it one bit.

The kitchen was alarmingly bright, clean dishes on the drying rack. A single cup in the sink. Candy picked up this glass and held it to the light. The tap leaked regularly as a clock.

Move it, Marty said.

Candy looked back over her shoulder, but from this part of the house, she couldn't see the front door where Marty stood guard.

That morning, he'd picked Candy up from the newspaper office like they'd agreed, and he said how sorry he was and that nothing like that would happen again and that it was over between him and Deborah and that he did certain things on account of his boy and then he asked Candy what was different about her. Something, he said, is different.

And Candy told him he was imagining things, that guilt could make a person see what wasn't there, and this part was true and nothing like what Candy said next about being the same, about being just how she always was.

Candy moved from the kitchen and down the hall, which was darker than any other part of the house. There were framed pictures there, mostly women from what Candy could tell, but in the shadows, all the portraits might have been the same person at different stages of her life. The same high forehead. The same sharp chin.

The first room Candy came to had been the old woman's. The bed was unmade and still a mess from the days the old woman had spent unattended. Marty said the paramedics said it was a miracle the lady didn't die.

There on the grandmother's dresser was a bud vase with the withered remains of what looked like small tree branches. The leaves had fallen around the bottom of the vase, a passing season in miniature.

Candy went on, further down the hall. The door at the end was closed, and Candy reached out, took hold of the cold knob, and pushed.

She'd had expectations, a collection of details she'd gleaned primarily from television shows. There would be a stereo. Posters. Dirty clothes under the bed. A drawer of stolen makeup.

But what Candy found was as neat as every other part of the house. The bed was covered in a yellow chenille spread that was straight and folded so as to cover the pillows. The closet door was shut, and when Candy opened it, she saw that all the clothes were hung or else folded and stacked on the top shelf. At the end of the rod were several formal dresses wrapped carefully in clear plastic.

Candy looked back down the hall to make sure this was the only other bedroom besides the grandmother's, which it was. But the room seemed like it didn't belong to any girl, like somebody had just stayed there.

There was no TV, no radio, no collection of tapes or CDs. There was, though, a little desk by the window. A silver soup can of pens and pencils and a stack of school books—*Algebra I, Health Today, English in the Modern World*.

Candy picked up the English book, flipped through the pages. She saw some familiar titles, but she hadn't read those stories in what seemed like a hundred years. Things were circled and underlined. There were notes in the margins. Bub sees what Robert sees, Makeisha had written at the end of the Carver story.

Marty was calling out to Candy.

Just a minute, Candy said.

With the other books was a library copy of *The Hidden Lives of Wolves*. It wasn't anything for biology class. That is, there weren't diagrams of skeletons and organs as in the book Candy had been studying. This book was more about wolf culture, community—clear color photographs of wolves running, wolves howling, wolves baring rows of sharp teeth.

What is it? Marty was saying.

And maybe this book hadn't been for a class, but Makeisha had studied it all the same. The pages were rippled and marked. Passages were underlined—*the modern study of wolves has revealed the true nature of the pack, and it is far less fanciful and far more familiar than many people had imagined.*

Candy turned the page. Certain pictures—mostly those of the lanky gray wolf pups—were circled with such force that Candy could feel the rut of the line beneath her thumb. She could feel the force of all that came behind it, of all that came before, and she could feel, too, her own blood pumping, a pulsing that came from her very core, and Marty was there now, and he was asking her what she'd found, and looking at him, Candy couldn't imagine what she'd ever seen in him, what she ever imagined to teach him or anyone else. It's nothing, Candy said, and Marty and everything in the room blurred and jerked and one thing could not, even by Candy, be told from another.

≈

Makeisha had drowned in Black Creek. This much they knew for certain. But they were still trying to determine the specifics, whether the drowning was accidental, suicidal, or, Marty said, otherwise. Too, they discovered that at the time of her death, Makeisha had been pregnant.

Marty gave Candy this news over the phone. He said, That last part, you can't print. Tonight. Corina's. Me and you.

Candy hung up the phone. On her desk was the book about wolves. She wasn't supposed to take it. She wasn't supposed to take anything, but she wasn't supposed to touch anything either. She'd hidden the book under her jacket, stuffed it halfway down the waist of her pants.

She read what Makeisha had read—all about wolves, their habitats, their predilections, the ways in which they were misunderstood. Candy had spent all that time trying to learn, trying to remember what all was on the inside, but now, what was left of the pancreas didn't seem to matter so much.

Candy read with her head in her hand, and with her brow hidden as it was, she looked like a child, and she was a child. She was a child and she was a forty-year-old woman, and in some way, Candy began to understand how she could become Makeisha, how she was Makeisha, how Marty was Makeisha, how Sue was Makeisha, how they all were Makeisha, and this didn't make sense exactly, but Candy saw now that hardly anything did. The truth was that reasons and methods and formulas had little business in the dealings of real people. Things happened in a way that didn't follow fixed charts and diagrams because when you got down to it, Mrs. Powell wasn't alone in the dark. They were all there with her, a kind of pack that moved together, that hunted together.

Candy saw now that she had no idea how to write this story or any other. Maybe the soap operas had it right after all. Maybe the purest form was a constant unraveling.

She felt sick, to be sure, but there was also a not altogether unpleasing levity. What a person might feel, for instance, after she's been gutted and what she's carried all this time has finally, if violently, been removed. What, in such a moment, might a person say?

Candy's hands trembled above the keys, and at last, after all these years, she really and truly began.

DRIVING LESSON

The storm had come and gone, but in the woods, there was still the impression, a steady and audible drip, an environmental trick the people here knew as tree rain. Water caught in the leaves and slowly funneled down into the fecund soil, and the dark creek swirled and eddied around a cypress knee, a washed down trash barrel, a chunk of road conglomerate. Because it was evening now, when the people came, the owl was startled into flight and flew the heft of himself from one tree to another, farther tree where his head swiveled and his eyes watched, and his feathers against that tree were a kind of cloak for disappearing.

The people made their way down the trail, and before this, they'd walked the length of Quinby Place because Quinby Place was where the girl had lived. Because this was where so many of them lived. And they'd met and gathered in the yard of Miss Miriam whose idea this was, who'd herself lost a daughter and a husband. And it was hot, especially so after the storm which did nothing to cool the day but charged it with a cruel humidity that collected on their necks and brows as if they were hard at labor and perhaps they were—the work of remembering what they would have preferred not to know in the first place. The people, the neighbors, longed for a glass of sweet tea, a conditioned breeze, a television court show. It was only human to want these things. Even, and perhaps especially, in their most noble moments that fought against the desires that governed one second and the next. They stood in the yard swatting mosquitoes and wanting what they could not have and do-ing their level best to consider what had been lost. This was important. This, mothers told their children, was serious.

They held their candles and did their best to shield the flames from what little wind their bodies created as they moved together down Quinby Place. And probably they should have sung. Probably Miss Miriam should have started them all on a worn-out hymn, but Miss Miriam's experience had taught her how little a song could matter, how much real silence was worth, and but for the occasion-al irrepressible scream of a child too young to understand memories, they moved without speaking, without much noise at all, and they did not wear dark clothes because it was hot and because this was no funeral. The funeral had been months ago.

They wore, without much thought, the light colors of summer, loose fabrics meant for breathing, and if Lonnie let her eyes fog over as she liked to do particularly when smoking, she could trick herself into thinking those peo-ple down below, those figures which moved with an un-usual and pointed solemnity were something altogether unworldly. The candle flames that danced and flickered. The pavement which, from the day's rain and heat, steamed with figures all its own which were like ghostly reflections of the people who walked.

Lonnie saw all of this from the roof of a house where she perched, one foot wedged against the brick chimney, with the bad guitarist who went by the name of Dots as in everything's a circle, man, as in everything's just one big black hole. It was this black hole, according to Dots, that was the beginning and the end to everything, to everyone. Some sooner than others.

Lonnie kicked at the chimney. You lied to me, she said. You're older than you say.

Dots had just taken a hit, and he choked on it now, wasting what was perfectly good. He tried to suck it back, puckered his lips and moved his head through the air like a vacuum cleaner in some demented world where machines were people and people were machines.

Lonnie watched him. I just want you to know. I want you to know that I know.

Dots had given up on the lost hit, and now he looked at Lonnie with a kind of half-smile. Right. Sure thing.

Lonnie stared down at the procession. There was this parade one time when I was a kid.

You're still a kid, Dots said and sat back against the chimney.

It was Christmas, Lonnie said, and there were these elves, these midgets throwing candy.

They don't like that word, Dots said. Midgets.

Those cinnamons in the red wrappers, Lonnie said.

Little persons. That's what they like.

And butterscotches.

It's all about being politically correct.

Hey, Lonnie said.

Yeah? Dots said.

And so these midgets were throwing these butter-scotches and these cinnamons. And I saw one and I went after it, and my daddy, he yanked me up so hard, my shoul-der pulled out of the socket.

Dots' head was back on his neck so all the loose skin of his throat hung in folds. Shit, he said.

Lonnie stared down at the ground where the little girl screamed at her mama to let her hold the candle.

I mean if you're a dude, Dots said.

It didn't hurt, Lonnie said. I mean I didn't feel it hurting.

Dots grunted. Most of the time, the weed did an all right job of keeping Dots on an even keel unless he got to thinking about his step-daddy, as he was just now. Lonnie could tell by the way his mouth twisted up under his nose.

That's the way it was, Dots said, when I broke my jaw.

Lonnie stared at the girl. Her mama had let her carry the candle, and now she was sticking her finger in the flame. She jerked her finger back. Then held it there longer.

This was different, Lonnie said.

Dots bit down on his lip.

There was a car backing up, Lonnie said, and I'd reached up under it.

Dots sort of laughed, mean-like, and looked at the joint. That is different, he said. Then he put the joint between his lips.

One of the women walking had a poster. It was a school picture made big and glued at the corners with blue plastic roses.

What good is this shit? Lonnie said. What good's any of it?

Dots took a bottle out of his back pocket. He unscrewed the lid, held it out to Lonnie.

Lonnie turned her head, and she wasn't looking at the picture anymore, but her face didn't change. She took the bottle. She reached for the joint. She smoked it.

So you told me one thing, Dots said.

He waited.

Lonnie rolled her lips. She held the smoke.

The people walked on, the crying girl with her finger in the flame, the woman and her homemade poster, the rest of them with their candles. It wasn't dark yet, but it would be soon.

After a while, after the people had gone down into the swamp, and the owl had heard them, and the owl had flown, and the moon was rising like a sun, Lonnie said, I need your help with something, and Dots said, Right. Sure thing.

≈

If a place were only trees and creek and rain running off the leaves, then the place had not changed at all. Even that very bridge under which they found the girl's body looked no different but for the flowers and the stuffed animals and the candles that would eventually go away to theft, to molder, to a trash-picking employee of the city who was finally told, It's time. And then the bridge, like the water that ran beneath it, would bear no marker of the tragedy that had occurred there, and people would have to work hard, they'd have to tell exaggerated stories to remind themselves what happened.

But place is not location. It isn't woods or creeks or owls or, in the case of Black Creek, what the rest of the country calls The Corridor of Shame. Place, like everything, is people, and the people who lived on Quinby Place, the people of Black Creek had, in a few months, changed in ways that were dramatic and permanent and if mirrored in the Earth's geology would have taken eons.

Black Creek was not a place where children died. At least that's what the people had thought even when circumstances said otherwise, and what changed about the people, about then, was that they realized that Black Creek *was* the kind of place where children died. Black Creek, like anywhere, was a little world unto its own, and with the girl they found in the water, they had, just before Christmas, buried the part of themselves that believed they were special, that they, in their world, were safe.

You can see it, Sarah said, in their faces.

She was down in the basement. She'd called for Lonnie to help her, which really meant she wanted Lonnie to sit on a stool in the corner, an out-of-the-way audience. Sarah was taking pictures again and not just for the school yearbook, not just to pay the bills. She was taking the kind of pictures she wanted to take, the kind of pictures, she told Lonnie, she took when she was young. She was starting, she said, to feel things again.

After your dad, Sarah said. Before that even.

Nothing Sarah said was clear or finished, and that had always, she said, been one of her biggest problems, but she was promising to try harder, she was promising to drink less, and she understood the way Lonnie saw her, the way, in fact, that Lonnie was looking at her, right then, during the sit-down Sarah called after she said she'd had some kind of epiphany out at Lake Darpo. She knew and understood what Lonnie thought about her, and she, Sarah, deserved that. She really did, but now she realized that she had a choice. She could either live or die.

She'd tried to say it as if the choice were obvious, but to Lonnie, it wasn't. To Lonnie, who'd once found her mother passed out on a near-lethal combination of drinks and pills, nothing was certain. Nothing could be trusted.

When you look at her face, Sarah said now, what do you see?

The photograph was taken down at the creek. A woman was on her knees on the bridge. She was looking out into the woods, like there was something there to see, like something was looking back at her.

Nothing, Lonnie said. I don't see shit.

Sarah kept her eyes on Lonnie, like she was waiting for something else. She took in air. She let it out. She said, I'm trying. I really am.

Lonnie stared at the floor.

Maybe you could try too, Sarah said.

Try what? Lonnie said.

Try talking, Sarah said. Try telling me what you think, how you feel. Tell me what's happening.

Lonnie looked up, and her eyes were dark and flat, and Sarah turned away. Sarah dropped the photograph and held onto the edge of the table. You can say, she said, what needs saying.

Lonnie stared at her mother, the knobs of her rounded back, the ridge of her knuckles. Sarah held the table like she was bracing for a hard hit, and Lonnie did want to hit her. She wanted to hit her as hard as she could, slap her across the face as she had that afternoon when she'd found her on the floor with her head under the foot of the bed. Lonnie had pulled her out by her arms, and it was instinct that pulled her hand back over her shoulder, that brought it down again across Sarah's powdered cheek, so hard, a foam of chalky spit sprayed against the wall, so hard, Lonnie felt her hand stinging as she dialed 9-1-1, as she held the phone against her own cheek, as she said, My mother's dead.

Even then, Lonnie knew that Sarah wasn't dead, but a part of her hoped that she was. A part of her wished she was dead, too. Everything was just so hard. An end, however it came, and whatever it brought next, seemed better than continuing.

Sarah held the table, and her shoulders moved up and down, and she said, We've gotta tell each other the truth. That's the only way this works.

Lonnie jumped up so quick, her heel shoved the stool against the wall, and Sarah jumped. Sarah squeezed her eyes shut.

Lonnie stared at her mother, at the sharp bones in her mother's neck. Then she turned and went up the stairs, two at a time. The truth is, she said, I'm fucking starving.

≈

Lonnie was starving. She was so hungry, she was dizzy, and the stairs, the walls, her room, the tree outside her window, a million leaves spun around her, but more and more, this was the world for Lonnie. More and more what was down was really up and what was up was really down, and everything that should have been right was wrong, wrong, wrong, and it was this sense of wrongness that made Lonnie want to hit her mother, this sense of injury and injustice that moved Lonnie to open her father's pocket knife, to make a short and careful cut just below her hip.

Sarah wanted the truth, but everything Lonnie could think of seemed like a lie, like something somebody had imagined.

Lonnie had changed too. That is, she was changing, so that even her own room seemed to belong to someone else, some girl who thought that if she tried hard enough, if she looked the right way and did the right things that were sometimes the wrong things, she might feel better. She might feel something.

There was so much Lonnie wanted, so much Lonnie needed. For a while, boys began to stand for it all, and Lonnie knew it wasn't boys exactly, but it was boys sort of, and so she'd worn the short shorts, and she'd flipped her hair, and she'd dragged Moto up and down the streets swishing and scoping, and they were searching, all right. They were looking as hard as they could, just not for the things that Lonnie claimed, and she'd wanted it. She'd wanted something. She'd wanted it so badly, she couldn't wait, and so she'd lied and said she'd done it already. She told Moto, made up some big story and all the details—what the room looked like, what he smelled like, how it felt, how, she'd said, everything had changed.

None of it was true. None of it was real.

Nothing, then, had changed. Lonnie's father was still dead. Her mother was still trying to die, and somewhere in a corner of every minute, Lonnie was still slapping Sarah, over and over again, a string of foam hanging in the air.

Now Moto was dead, and though the world spun as it always had, Lonnie saw it from some different place. She saw it for what it was, an ugly wobbling blur of dirt and smoke and fire and flash, and like Sarah, Lonnie wanted the truth. She wanted some kind of justice, some sense of reason and purpose. She wanted to hear something besides her own heart beating, and if you wanted something to happen, if you wanted more than a made-up story, you had to do it yourself. You had to open the knife. You had to press the blade until something broke, and then, at least for a minute, things would be right again.

Lonnie made the cuts, and on her hip was a score, as if there could be some kind of victory in adding up all that she'd lost. When it was done, she went to the window, and on the other side of it, the leaves were still and no rain fell and she called Dots. She told him to get what they needed. She told him to be ready.

≈

When Moto figured out she was pregnant—and, because she was fifteen and, in some ways, a young fifteen, it *was* a sort of figuring, a slow progress of problem-solving as if the body had a complicated code that needed to be broken—Lonnie was the first to know.

Moto didn't, wouldn't, say who she'd been with, but Lonnie figured it out soon enough, and when it hit her, when she came to that small and ugly awareness, there was also a larger sort of irrevocable knowledge that both girls sensed more than understood, and they stared, they looked hard at the space between them that seemed, just then, to widen until it was as broad as the streets they'd spent so much time walking together. Looking, Sarah said, for trouble.

There's a tea you can drink, Lonnie said. She'd heard some of the pretty girls talking in the bathroom. They hadn't known she was in the stall or else they would have zipped up their makeup bags and cartwheeled away from that yucky girl who was always trying to make the team, who was always following them around like some kind of stalker. And it was sad that her dad was dead and her mom, the lady who took their cheerleading picture, was crazy, batshit crazy, they said, but that didn't mean you could act however you wanted. That didn't mean you could walk around looking like a slut.

Herbs, Lonnie said, or something.

Moto didn't know what she would do, and it turned out, there wasn't enough time to find out because a few weeks later, they'd found her in the swamp. They found her floating on her back in the creek, and if a person didn't know better and didn't look close, she might think the girl had just went in the water. Maybe she was just floating there, so intent on finding faces in the clouds that she didn't answer when they called. She didn't even blink.

After they'd found her, after they'd pulled her out of the water, the cops had come around Quinby Place. And some lady from the newspaper. They had all sorts of questions, but Moto had made Lonnie promise not to say, and after everything, it seemed it was the least Lonnie could do. She said she didn't know anything, and for once, Sarah understood something in Lonnie's face, something about the situation, and told them to go away, to leave her daughter alone, to let them grieve in peace.

I just want to scare him a little, Lonnie told Dots that day they were on the roof, the day of the memorial. I just want to rattle his cage.

Yeah, Dots said. Dots himself spent a lot of his stoned time developing intricate and alternate revenge plots. He rubbed his chin. Sure thing.

The man—David was his name—lived on Quinby Place, just a few houses down from Lonnie and her mother. Quinby Place was at the edge of the swamp, and most of the houses were surrounded by encroaching thickets of bushes and vines and junk trees that people spent a lot of time trimming and cutting and shaping into what they called wind breaks. They weren't fences exactly, but they separated the houses, and so afforded each neighbor a friendly measure of privacy. It was in this thicket that Lonnie and Dots hid.

The curtains were closed at the front of the house, but on the side, they could see right through to the kitchen table where David hunched over a small piece of wood and a thin paintbrush.

He builds planes, Lonnie said. The air conditioner came on, and the leaves in the trees moved around them. David's windows were closed, but all the same, Lonnie was careful to keep her voice down.

Dots sniffed and raked a hand under his nose. Planes, he said. Like jets?

Lonnie shook her head. No, like toys.

Dots blinked. He squeezed his eyes shut and then opened them again. He did this twice, like it was something he couldn't help, like he couldn't focus. Models, he said. Model planes.

Yeah, Lonnie said. Those.

Dots snorted, and Lonnie thought he was laughing, but when Lonnie looked—she could see Dots in the other-world haze of the streetlight—he wasn't smiling. She said, Something's wrong with you.

Dots shook his head. Then he looked at Lonnie and said, I'm fine.

Whatever was wrong with Dots was always wrong with Dots, but he'd done something, taken something to make it even worse. The muscles in his neck jumped, and beside Lonnie, he felt very nearly electric.

Twisted freak, Dots said. He was talking about David, about the story Lonnie told about David and Moto and what happened between them and then what might have happened between them because really, she didn't know. Really, Lonnie didn't know any more than anybody else because Moto had drowned, that much was certain, but they couldn't figure out exactly why or how. They thought somebody might have drowned her, but then they also thought she might have drowned herself, and when Moto went missing, Lonnie was so caught up in herself, so worried about what she was going do and why that she couldn't say for sure one way or another whether her best friend would have done something like that. There was a time when she would have said her mother wouldn't have, that her mother had something to live for, but that hadn't stopped her from trying.

It's time to set things right, Dots said. Nobody's doing it for us. Isn't that what you said?

Through the glass, David looked like a big bald baby working on some art project. His tongue was stuck out and wrapped around his upper lip.

I don't know, Lonnie said. She'd been sure before, but now she wasn't.

Huh?

I said I don't know.

You don't know what?

It's just—

Dots was watching her. His face was close to her own, and Lonnie could hear, she could practically feel his teeth grinding.

Maybe we shouldn't, Lonnie said.

Sure we should. We are.

We're not yet.

I am.

Lonnie looked at him. The streetlight made shadows of his face, the jaw which worked and worked. She'd started something in him, and she couldn't turn it off.

You know how old I am, Dots said, and he pulled the mask down over his face. And I've been working at this my whole life.

≈

Lonnie told Dots that story about the parade, the candy, her shoulder out of place. Her father, like Moto, was dead. Her mother had tried to die. Lonnie herself almost got run over while a marching band, in near-perfect formation, played "Jingle Bell Rock."

You want to get yourself killed? her father said. See what happens. See what happens when you don't listen.

But Lonnie *was* listening. She'd heard the squawk of the trumpet. The horns of the clown cars. The horse clatter and the crack of thrown candy. There was something else though. There had to be something she'd missed.

He was angry, but in the hospital, he touched her face, he touched her hair, and his fingers were so light, she could barely feel them, the way they shook, the pounding in his chest when he held her so long, so tight, the nurse told him to leave, to wait outside because, she said, children didn't do as well when their parents were around.

There was a narrow window in the door, and through the glass, Lonnie watched her father. She saw him mouth words, something else she couldn't hear. There was so much she didn't understand. Dots said she wasn't stupid. She just didn't know anything. She was just a kid.

Didn't she get it? Didn't she see the way that once something broke, you couldn't put it back together?

And Lonnie, trying to calm him down, trying to talk sense, said, Nothing's broke, Dots. It's all together. One big circle, right? No beginning, no end.

And Dots nodded, but it wasn't anything that made anybody but him feel better. That's the problem, he said. That's it exactly.

And then Lonnie saw the gun, and she wanted to believe the gun, like the planes, like the models, was a toy, something that, like everything in Lonnie's world, was completely unreal, and how was it that she felt for David? How was it that she and Dots both saw in him their own fathers? Not the day he'd pulled her shoulder out of socket, but another time in the hospital, years later when he was full of cancer, and the night before he died, while Lonnie studied for a Spanish quiz, while she memorized words in some meaningless chant, his face changed, like he was seeing something. Like he was accepting whatever it was he saw.

And Dots was running and so was Lonnie. She was running before she knew she was running. Out from the bushes and down the street she'd walked so many times with Moto because there was nothing to do. There was never anything a person could do. She saw that now.

Her house, up the stairs, to the room, her heart beating like any other heart, a thing in a cage that can be measured and timed by a machine, a *beep-beep* that somehow equals life until it doesn't.

Dots was right. She didn't know anything, so what could she tell her mother? Where would she even start on a Saturday morning when Sarah was getting her out of bed, when Sarah was so obviously trying to get her shit together, and saying, Come on. Let's go. Hurry up.

Where? was all Lonnie could say.

And Sarah said, I know a place. I'll show you.

≈

As it turned out, where they were going didn't matter as much as how they were getting there. At the edge of town, by a string of warehouses and shut-up businesses, Sarah pulled over. She didn't cut the engine, but she got out, walked around to Lonnie's side, and opened the door.

Your turn, she said.

Lonnie was nearly sixteen, and it was time. It was past time, Sarah said.

Lonnie moved mechanically, automatically. Her body was a bundle of wires.

It wasn't that she didn't think about David and what might have happened to him as much as it was this very thought, the vision of him in the window and Dots and the gun, that had appeared and then exploded, shutting out, shorting out everything else.

The engine idled as Lonnie walked around the back of the car and slid behind the wheel.

Sarah was in the passenger seat, and she said, The first thing you do is adjust your mirrors. Make sure you can see all around you.

Lonnie moved the mirrors. She caught sight of herself and looked away quick.

Sarah said, Put your foot on the break when you change gear.

Lonnie did what Sarah said, and Sarah said to press on the gas. Slow, she said. Easy.

And like that, they were moving.

Keep both hands on the wheel, Sarah said. At all times.

Lonnie stared ahead.

It's scary at first, Sarah said.

Yeah, Lonnie said.

For years, she and Moto had talked about all the things they'd do, all the places they'd go when they got a car, when they could finally drive. Lonnie held the wheel. She felt the engine through the plastic, the power of it. She felt a part of the car and the space it cut through the swamps.

For a while, they were quiet. Black Creek was behind them, and yet it was in all the mirrors. It was everywhere around Lonnie, and in some way, it always would be even if all she heard was the sound of the road against the tires, a kind of low roar that Dots said was the beginning and end of everything.

Where is it? Lonnie said. You were gonna show me a place.

She didn't look at her mother, afraid as she was to take her eyes off the road and afraid, too, that if she looked at her mother, she might really see something, and so, even now, when her mother is gone, and Lonnie is alone, she sees the swamps and the road out, but it's her mother's voice saying, It's here. It's everywhere.

BIOGRAPHICAL NOTE

Landon Houle's writing has won contests at *Black Warrior Review*, *Crab Creek Review*, *Dogwood*, and *Permafrost*. Other work has appeared in *Baltimore Review*, *Crazyhorse*, *Natural Bridge*, *Harpur Palate*, *River Styx*, *The New Guard*, and elsewhere. Landon was born in Brown County, Texas, and currently lives in Darlington, South Carolina. She is an assistant professor of English and creative writing at Francis Marion University, and she is the fiction editor at *Raleigh Review*.